D1229922

SONS OF THE CLOUDS

SONS OF THE CLOUDS

Marcel G. Laugel

in collaboration with
Robert de Sadow

Philosophical Library
New York

Library of Congress Cataloging-in-Publication Data

Laugel, Marcel G.
  Sons of the clouds.

  1. Tindouf Region (Algeria)—History—
Fiction.   I. Title.
PR9105.9.L38S6   1986   823'.914   85-16768

ISBN 8022-2479-2
Copyright 1987 by Philosophical Library, Inc.
200 West 57th Street, New York, N.Y. 10019.
All rights reserved.
Manufactured in the United States of America.

To General Pigeot. *In Memoriam.*

To Françoise, Anne and François.

A NOTE TO THE READER

This book is a biographical novel based on events that occurred in the late 1950s in the westernmost part of the Sahara, when the French Colonial Army and the natives were competing for predominance in this area.

The boundaries of this territory were roughly marked by the River Drâa, along the Moroccan border to the North, by the Tabelbala oasis to the east, by the ridge of the Hank to the south, and by the Atlantic Ocean to the west (Map 3).

Generally speaking, this period has not always been fully understood by world public opinion, which is inclined to associate colonialism with repression and war. This account describes the efforts made by the French Colonial Administration to keep peace and avoid bloodshed while having the French and native laws respected.

The two heroes are Major Larcher and Chieftain Salah. Larcher is an army officer, endowed with humanistic qualities and great knowledge, who fought in the anti-Nazi campaign in France and later in the Vietnam war. Over the years, while riding on his camel throughout the French Sahara, he found many opportunities to use his capacities as a warrior and his talents as a negotiator. He had established his headquarters at Tindouf.

Salah belonged to the native Bedouin aristocracy, generally referred to as "the Great Tents"—in the same way as people would say "the Great Families" when mentioning European aristocracy. He came in direct line from a saint named Sid Ahmed Reguibi, clever at war and politics, who, by the end of the 17th century, had succeeded in unifying all the nomadic tribes scattered over the area. In return, these tribes as a whole were named for him, "the Reguibat."

The Reguibat Confederation consisted of two major ethnic groups, one originating in the west and called Sahel Reguibat, the other coming from the east named the Legouacem Reguibat. Although differentiated by their geographical origins, both groups were organized on the same sociological pattern, based on the feudal concept of slavery. Each group, therefore, was subdivided into two categories, the richer and the poorer tribes, the latter serving as the slaves of the former. In other words, slavery was the basis of the Reguibat economy.

Logically enough, Salah, who thought of himself as the legal chief of the Reguibat, declared himself against the French occupation and the enforcement of French law based on the principles of liberty, equality, fraternity. By the time the French came in he had succeeded in gaining the upper hand over some semi-nomadic and sedentary tribes living within his territory. Such was the case with the Tajakant, who had settled in the Tindouf oasis (Map 3). Salah was a powerful political chief but also a religious leader. He therefore had two good reasons for opposing the French. They were Christians—that is, infidels—and they would forbid the practice of slavery, which meant the ruin of the Reguibat economy. He thus decided to prevent them from ruling his country.

His tactics, which consisted of avoiding any contact between his people and the French, proved successful for a while. At length however, the lesser tribes came to realize that French liberalism could help them liberate themselves from their over-lords, and they decided to seize that chance. Such powerful tribes as the Sidi Allal and the Belgacem ou Brahim gradually lost their influence over such groups as the Sellam and the Foqra, who used to serve as their camelherders. Thus the Reguibat economy started to decline, since camel breeding was the main source of income of the Reguibat. The proclamation of the independence of neighboring Morocco in 1956 had a great effect on Salah's life and the life of the Reguibat.

I have attempted to tell the story of Salah the Reguibat while at the same time providing detailed information on the nomadic way of life in the Western Sahara of the late 1950s. This book is based on a wide range of experiences I went through during my six years of service in the Reguibat Terri-tory. During that time, as an officer in the French Colonial Army, I served as an interpreter to the officer portrayed as Larcher.

MGL

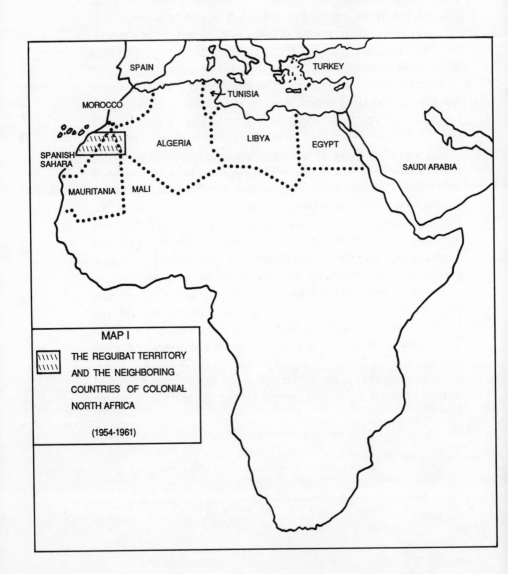

SPAIN

TURKEY

MOROCCO

TUNISIA

SPANISH
SAHARA

ALGERIA

LIBYA

EGYPT

SAUDI ARABIA

MAURITANIA

MALI

MAP I

THE REGUIBAT TERRITORY
AND THE NEIGHBORING
COUNTRIES OF COLONIAL
NORTH AFRICA

(1954-1961)

CHRONOLOGY

1934:	French rule starts at Tindouf.
November 5, 1955:	Sultan Mohammed V returns to Morocco from exile.
March 2, 1956:	Independence of Morocco.
March 12, 1957:	General de Gaulle visits Tindouf.
February 1958:	"Ecouvillon" Operation. Joint expedition by the French and Spanish armies in Mauritania and Rio de Oro. Rebel Reguibat rally to France.
November 28, 1960:	Independence of Mauritania.
March 1, 1961:	Death of Sultan Mohammed V. Sultan Hassan II ascends the throne.
March, 17, 1961:	Announcement of negotiations between France and the FLN (Algerian Liberation Front) which lead to the proclamation of the independence of Algeria on July, 3, 1962.

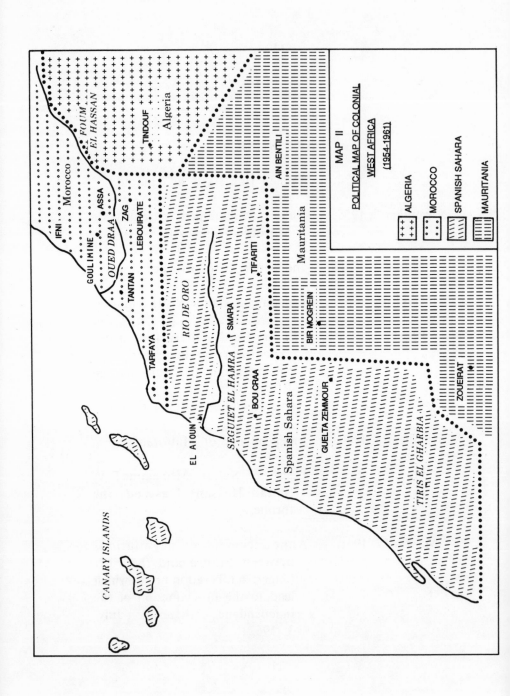

MAP II

POLITICAL MAP OF COLONIAL
WEST AFRICA
(1954-1961)

+++ +++	ALGERIA
· · · ·	MOROCCO
\\\\\\	SPANISH SAHARA
‖‖‖‖	MAURITANIA

CANARY ISLANDS

IFNI · Morocco
GOULIMINE
ASSA
OUED DRAA
ZAG
TANTAN
LEBOUIRATE
TARFAYA
RIO DE ORO
EL AIOUN
SEGUIET EL HAMRA
SMARA
BOU CRAA
Spanish Sahara
GUELTA ZEMMOUR
BIR MOGREIN
TIFARITI
AIN BENTILI
Mauritania
TIRIS EL GHARBIA
ZOUEIRAT

FOUM
EL HASSAN
TINDOUF
Algeria

GEOGRAPHICAL BACKGROUND
RELEVANT TO THE UNFOLDING OF THE STORY

Tindouf: located approximately 500 km. Southeast of Agadir (Map 3).

   8° 11′ ii″ West Longitude
   27° 43′ 43″ North Latitude

Tindouf lies - 40 km. from the Rio de Oro Border.

   - 120 km. from the Moroccan Border.

   - 1000 km. from the city of Colomb Béchar, Algeria (approximately).

   - 350 km. from the City of Ain Ben Tili, Mauritania (approximately).

   - 700 km. from the city of Smara, Rio de Oro (approximately).

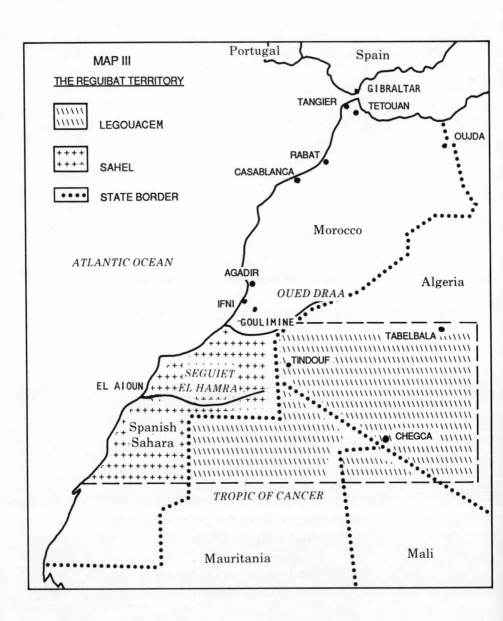

MAP III

THE REGUIBAT TERRITORY

\\\\\ LEGOUACEM

++++
++++ SAHEL

•••• STATE BORDER

Portugal   Spain

GIBRALTAR

TANGIER   TETOUAN

OUJDA

RABAT

CASABLANCA

Morocco

Algeria

ATLANTIC OCEAN

AGADIR

IFNI   OUED DRAA

GOULIMINE

TABELBALA

TINDOUF

SEGUIET

EL AIOUN   EL HAMRA

Spanish

Sahara   CHEGCA

TROPIC OF CANCER

Mauritania   Mali

TRIBES

The plot of the novel involves the Legouacem Reguibat only.

The tribe of Brahim ou Daoud—issued from Kacem the son of Sid Ahmed Reguibi—was divided into the following subtribes:

- Sidi Allal,
- Belgacem ou Brahim,
- Selalka,
- Jenha,
- Lahcen ou Ahmed.

For many centuries they have kept these other tribes under their control:

- Sellam,
- Oulad Sid Ahmed,
- Foqra.

Women at the well before departure

PROLOGUE

He was coming from the south looking for some lost camels. Later he planned to join his father's encampment farther to the north. He had stopped at the well at Bir Lefjah to replenish his water bottle and water his camel. Scarcely had he finished when a group of five young Sellam, about his own age, arrived on the scene. Upon recognizing him, they began to hurl insults. Not wanting to risk a fight in which he would have been outnumbered, Mahmoud decided to move a distance away to make his tea. As a precaution he had left his camel saddled with its hind legs tethered so that it would not wander off. As an extra precaution he had also slipped a bullet into his rifle to enable a rapid return of fire.

The Sellam only increased their threats. Two of them were armed. He preferred to be vigilant but it was necessary that his camel rest a few hours until the sun set once more and he was able to resume his journey.

One of the five Sellam, Mohammed ould Souilem, the most brazen, approached and sat down opposite him. A curious dialogue ensued. Mohammed again took up his taunts but Mahmoud interrupted:

"How can you hurl such insults at an armed man when you are not armed?"

"Because I know that you are a coward and have no more idea how to use a gun than a woman."

"Do you know that for this insult I can kill you?"

"Yes, but my companions are armed and would kill you in turn."

"At least I would die with honor."

"The Sidi Allal are without honor. They are our exploiters and former masters and only deserve our hate."

"Do you know that with my loaded gun I can end your life?"

"With you I risk nothing. I despise you. May Allah devastate your tent and that of your poor little father."

Mahmoud, maddened with rage, fired straight at his taunter. A target only six feet away posed no challenge to his marksmanship. Mohammed died instantly. Then Mahmoud ran for his nearby camel, springing into the saddle expertly, at the same time releasing the tether. The victim's companions, who had been alerted at the sound of the shot, ran after in hot pursuit. One of them fired two or three shots in Mahmoud's direction, but the bullets fell short as the camel surged forward.

Mahmoud rode all night and all the next morning without eating or drinking.

IMPORTANT CHARACTERS

Major Larcher, commander of the French garrison at Tindouf
General Pignon, his superior
Lieutenant Vogel, one of Larcher's officers
Lieutenant de La Renaudie, one of Larcher's officers
Lieutenant de Vignandeau, one of Larcher's officers
Lieutenant Blizzard, one of Larcher's officers
Salah ould Ahmed, chief of the Sidi Allal, spiritual leader of
    the Legouacem Confederation, considers himself chief of
    the Reguibat
Ahmed, his oldest son
Mahmoud, his youngest son
Meriem, his first wife
Salambouha, his second wife
Minatou, his old servant
Hassan ould Bouali, chief of the Belgacem ou Brahim
Hamoudi ould Himdoun, chief of the Sellam
Ghit ould Bouaha, Hamoudi's counsellor
Ali ould Abdi, leader of the Lachen ou Ahmed
Lemjed ould Bara, leader of the Foqra
Mantallah ould Senhouri, a caravaneer, mayor of the Taja-
    kant village
Zein ould Himed, a cameleer
Fatimatou, his wife
Minatou, his beloved
Mokhtar, his father-in-law
Mohammed V, King of Morocco

19

Mosq of Tindouf viewed from palm trees

CHAPTER I

Larcher was pressed against the window of his office gazing with total absorption. A veil of dust blanketed the village of Tindouf, which had been besieged by the sandstorm for many days. Squalls of southwesterly winds were agitating the foliage of the palm trees. The sun, already high in the sky, was too weak to penetrate the layer of dust suspended in the air, although its rays imparted a milky luminescence to the square inside the fort. At times one could barely make out the columns of the buildings in long rows, the sand advancing wave after wave upon their bases. Segments of domes appeared briefly through windblown dust, revealing their 1930s colonial architecture. It seemed as though life itself had stopped. From time to time a solitary man, his head completely wrapped, proceeded dutifully from one building to another, staggering against the blustering wind. The tempest billowed his tunic until it resembled a filled waterskin, and his silhouette from afar seemed strikingly comical.

One consequence of these common gales, which sometimes persisted for an entire month, was an increased level of irritability among the men. It was a time of anger and quarrels. A feeling of ill-humor permeated everyone at the fort, from the lowest-ranking soldiers all the way up to the commanding officers. Yet Larcher steadfastly managed to retain his composure, standing out noticeably from the rest. He always found in these storms a soothing seduction that was vaguely surrealistic.

It was no great hardship for the soldiers though, in this tranquil climate with its perpetually clear blue sky, to be occasionally subjected to the elements. All things, both large and small, collected dust. Its incessant accumulation had to be tolerated, since any attempt to clear it was insufficient at best. After a while the dust became no more unpleasant than rain or snow.

Larcher thought of the discomfort of his Meharist half-companies out in the desert. He reminisced about how he had been in the same predicament ten years earlier, his head covered by a cowl and his feet by loose-fitting sandals. He remembered the sting of the wind-driven sand, as it was propelled at high speed. In vain he had attempted to make shelter utilizing his saddle and a sheep skin. His camel had decided to ride out the storm in his own way by resting on the ground, stretching his long, snakelike neck in the soil to offer less resistance to the hostile wind. It was usually impossible to start and maintain a fire, so it became necessary to use a paste made of dates as food. Although highly nourishing, the paste developed a characteristic crunchiness because of the sand and the frequent transfer from the left hand to the right hand. While waiting for a break in the weather, Larcher had munched on his ration to stave off hunger.

Now he paused in his reflections and returned to his desk. He moved a file within reach, blowing off some of the accumulated sand and dust and immersed himself once again in deep study. However, his concentration failed him, and Larcher quickly closed the file again. His thoughts wandered. "Here I am, chief of the battalion, a twenty-year veteran, and now I have been given this ludicrous task to perform. I only hope my superiors know what they are doing." He shifted on his chair and packed tobacco into his pipe and placed it in his mouth unlighted. He recalled his visit to Colomb-Béchar a month earlier, vividly picturing his superior. General Pignon had decided to brief him on what was about to unfold. Pignon was a small man, alert, with penetrating eyes behind metal-rimmed spectacles. The general was not one for circumlocutions. His language was precise and near-metallic, a habit he had developed from years of issuing commands to his troops.

Because he had been among the first officers to lead the Meharist troops of Tindouf in 1934, the general had an easy familiarity with the native people of the borderland flanked by Algeria, Mauritania, and Morocco. Pignon was concerned by the current situation. Morocco had been expectantly awaiting its independence, and this had produced a period of turmoil . The turmoil had then spread to Algeria. Nothing had happened as yet in this borderland area flanked by Algeria, Mauritania, and Morocco—a territory half the measure of France. But there was one prestigious Bedouin chief who possesed a "sense of ground." In other words, he knew the political geography of the territory. This Bedouin had displayed an attitude that was not easily interpreted; it was either a posture of indignant self-defense or a new tactic of resistance. "Your mission involves only one task," said Pignon summarily. "You must make this old man publicly submit to our authority. He is either a cunning fox or an irascible fool. I leave the choice to you, Larcher, after you have studied his strategy. From this you can ascertain the man's psychology and character. But beware of simplifications, presumptions, and analyses that are too hastily drawn. I know the Bedouins well. I have met them often. And I am inclined to think that this one cannot be easily characterized; he does not fit into a standard mold. Sometimes one must probe more deeply into the psyche of such a man without taking the easier and more obvious route."

The two men parted under the patio's archway fronting the now-deserted camel square. It was illuminated by dazzling shafts of sunlight. Wafts of heated vapor ascended from the hilly ground. Larcher remembered that moment. He had said very little, choosing mainly to listen to Pignon. He had wondered what sort of impression he was making on his commanding officer.

It so happened that Pignon's impression of Larcher was favorable. Pignon appreciated the bearing of this physically appealing man who was of middle height with a strong neck and well-developed shoulders. Larcher displayed a prominent and powerful jaw which nonetheless did nothing to mar the serenity of his face. Two deep black eyes glanced easily about, alternating between moments of tranquility and quiet determination. Pignon felt convinced that the Bedouin chieftain, Salah ould Ahmed, would view this new head of Tindouf as a worthy opponent.

CHAPTER II

Larcher's mission seemed to be purely routine. All he had to do was place a red wool cloak on the shoulders of a nomadic chieftain. The long sleeveless garment, known as a *burnoose*, was actually a great honor from the French authorities. In a way it symbolized a feudal ceremony, with a vassal's pledge of loyalty to his sovereign before an assembly of notables. The practice had proven to be good politics. The administration found nomadic chieftains to be qualified spokesmen for their tribes, an arrangement that pleased the tribal chiefs themselves. They saw it as an additional way to reinforce their positions over people that traditionally opposed authority.

Ceremony of "red Burnoose" in the court of garrison of Tindouf.

For the first time, however, in the twenty years that France had occupied the region, one leader in the Reguibat faction had refused to go along. Reading Salah's file was a disappointment. Secondhand information had been brought back by youthful opportunists who were willing to help in systematically destroying the old man. Salah seemed to be a leader in his waning years in whom stubbornness, vanity, and craftiness had become predominant. In short, he seemed to be a rather unattractive personage, the guardian of anachronistic traditions and resistant to any kind of social change.

Although Salah had avoided saying or doing anything that spoke of rebellion, he had refused to present himself to French authorities. By remaining aloof, he had interfered with French intentions.

This state of affairs had already persisted for five years and it was clearly time to come to an end. It was all the more urgent that talks be conducted with Salah since he exercised charismatic power over the entire confederation.

He was the direct descendant of the man who had founded the Reguibat, a confederation that extended to Sahel in the west and Legouacem in the east. He was the spiritual heir of the great Ahmed Reguibi, a holy man of the eighteenth century who by his courage and vision had succeeded in uniting the nomadic tribes into a vast empire. According to oral traditions, Ahmed had defined a territory bordered on the north by the course of the Wed Dra, the natural frontier with mountainous Morocco, and to the east by a line separating this river from the oasis of Tabelbala, the extreme point of the settlements of the Negroid Berbers. Hank Cliff was the geographic barrier marking the southern limit of this quadrilateral, which ended in the west with the seventh wave of the ocean. Sid Ahmed Reguibi had formulated this peculiar idea of "territorial waters." He had hoped that the shark-free space within these seven waves, tantamount to an inhospitable barrier, would be an ideal spot for ambushes of passing ships. The resulting shipwrecks would then become the property of the coastal people. Ahmed had shown a political genius similar to Youseff Ibn Tachfin, the founder of the Almoravides, who had left a fortified convent in Senegal as a way station for journeys to Seville. He had laid the foundations of a nomadic state between two sedentary peoples.

This history gave Larcher better insight into the personality of Salah ould Ahmed. How could one reproach the spiritual leader of all the Reguibat for being indifferent to a ceremonial red cloak? Perhaps the whole issue could be circumvented if Salah were asked to confine himself to his religious role. The experts however, were adamant that the formal political ceremony take place. They pointed out that Islam spiritual and temporal power were combined. Therefore Salah could remain true to his beliefs while still accepting the cloak.

Larcher felt as though he were caught in a whirlpool. He knew that the other nomadic tribes were watching this silent duel between an all-powerful French administration and their leader. Of course, to quote an Arab proverb, "Patience is the key to mercy," but patience could not last forever. Somehow or other, communication had to be established between Salah and the ruling power.

But by what means? Send a camel troop? It would give the officer in charge a good opportunity to meet with the old man. But how would Salah react to the arrival of eighty armed men? He might be warm and friendly, putting on a feast as only nomads can when they are so disposed. And he'd use the occasion to score points, sacrificing several camels, to the utter delight of men who had been without meat for months on end. But, amid the general atmosphere of euphoria, he might also make disparaging remarks about the soldiers.

Larcher considered another possibility. Salah might refuse to accommodate the French officer while at the same time offering hospitality to his men. That would be an insult difficult to accept. Knowing nothing of the psychology of the man in question, Larcher thought it might be better to do nothing.

But then an alternative course of action came to mind. Why not choose a handful of men for a patrol? During their routine tour of duty, a census count for example, they might arrive at the leader's camp quite by chance. The commander of such a patrol could be none other than the young Lieutenant Vogel, who served as interpreter. He had the advantage of understanding and speaking the local dialect known as *Hassaniya*, studying it with all the enthusiasm of a newcomer. But he was lacking in experience and Salah would not take him seriously. Better keep this young man out of such an operation and avoid the possibility of his being discredited in the eyes of these people. Vogel's knowledge of the language and terrain would be invaluable in the service of his country at a later date.

After mulling this problem over, Larcher came up with another plan. Suppose he had the nomads come to the administrative capital. But the journey had to be made worth their while. He decided to resurrect the "spring fairs" which his predecessor had let lapse. They were a sort of agricultural show that local people referred to as *choufan*, a gathering that would serve more than one purpose. The French influence was being contested in Algeria as well as Morocco so it was vital that France present itself in a confident and capable manner. In addition, Larcher shrewdly reasoned that it would give him an opportunity to see Salah and to make acquaintance of his people before one of Salah's lieutenants could be dispatched as an observer of the new administration's forces.

Ceremony of "red Burnoose" outside of Tindouf in nomadic area.

CHAPTER III

A high-pitched trill, coming from behind residential terraces, pinpointed the troop's relative position in the oasis. The characteristic sound, made by a rapid tongue movement against the roof of the palate, was a customary greeting offered by women welcoming back their husbands, brothers, and friends after a six-month absence. The camel corps, following an established route, emerged from the palm plantations to the south of the first houses in the eastern section of the town. Uncertain at first, the joyful clamoring drew nearer, culminating at the residence of the *Caid*. By this time it was clear that at any moment the three mounted units would be reaching the

31

open space between the administrative fort and the town, an expanse vast enough for parades.

Larcher, in a blue *kepi* (cap), officer's white tunic, and baggy black trousers, rode alone at the head of his men. He executed the regulation about-turn and ordered the foot-soldier captain to present arms. The sound of rifles sliding from shoulder to hip height and the slap of hands on wooden barrels showed that these were well-trained, seasoned soldiers. Larcher enjoyed watching the movement performed in unison as if by one man. The silence that followed in the ranks seemed to emphasize the immobility of men turned temporarily to stone.

The senior lieutenant, de Vignandeau, led the parade. Perched on his tall, white camel, the officer tried to keep to an imaginary straight line. Behind him rode the seventy men of his unit in columns of three. The camels moved forward at a slow trot, their long heads held high, their expression disdainful. They clip-clopped down the dusty road on long, ungainly legs and soft, spreading feet, sounding like a chorus of dancers on a wooden floor. All the animals seemed to be superlatively conditioned. Gelded dromedaries, standing well over six feet high at the shoulder, they had been selected for the camel corps only after rigorous inspection. Now, with coats glistening, they loped by with an air of triumph and the faint detachment known only to racing animals that outshine their fellows.

The camel corps presented a proud appearance. If the soldiers were Arabs from the East, they wore tall red *chéchias* on their heads; in the case of the Moors, the attire consisted of blue robes and black *chéches* with prominent red-leather cartridge belts sporting brass shells. Their left hands guided the camels with a single rein attached to rings in the animals' nostrils. Their right hands held rifles which rested on the edge of their saddles. Though their bodies swayed as they rode, their heads remained nearly motionless. When he passed the commander, de Vignandeau shouted "eyes right" to the troop and saluted, swinging his right hand up to his *kepi*, his fingers

The Camel Corps

wide apart in the elite style affected by the cavalry officers. His platoon was followed by that of de La Renaudie, a slim silhouette on a particularly tall camel that he rode gracefully. Bringing up the rear was Lieutenant Blizzard, a red-headed giant whose own gangling legs and arms only seemed to emphasize the shuffling, irregular gait of his camel. Larcher reprimanded him with a smile on his lips. The lieutenant was a long way from the rice-field in Tonkin where Larcher had once seen him heroically lead his men across a dike under machine gun fire. How many bridges had been traversed that way by young officers! For a fleeting moment he thought sadly of those who were now dying on those same dikes in a meaningless war. Larcher was proud of his young lieutenants, all three of whom had survived two tours of duty in Vietnam and had earned the Legion of Honor under fire.

They would probably talk about the unceasing conflict in the mess hall this evening.

Once past the parade ground, the units disappeared behind the plantations. The day had started well with the sun already high in the sky. However, the heat was still bearable due to the faint breeze that wafted over the *hamada* at this time of the year. Larcher summoned Vogel.

"The reception for the designated chiefs is at ten o'clock, isn't it?"

"Ten-thirty sir."

"Well?"

"Everything seems to be going all right. The sheikhs responded to our invitation."

"Will all the tribes be represented?" asked Larcher casually.

"All of them. Even the sub-groups."

"That means then that the Sidi Allal will be there?"

"Yes, but Salah is sick and has sent his son Ahmed to represent him."

The two men exchanged knowing smiles, Larcher realizing that he had guessed correctly. All the chiefs had come, prompted by curiosity and interest. Even Salah could not resist such an occasion but he had predictably sent his son—with two aims in mind. He intended to convince his opposition, particularly the Sellam, that his absence was deliberate, and also that his direct heir could thwart any moves favorable to the administration. He intended to show that the entire confederation was indisputably subject to his authority.

On Larcher's arrival the chiefs rose as a body from the rugs on which they had been squatting in his spacious office. After a ringing *Sallam Alikum* by the assemblage, Larcher shook hands as he proceeded to the left side of the room. Vogel introduced each sheikh by his tribal origin. Proper protocol was dispensed with as a precautionary measure, allowing for customary alignments of political currents in the disparate Reguibat-Legouacem confederation. The allied Sidi Allal and Belgacem ou Brahim were opposed by the more closely knit Sellam and Foqra. The poorest members were on equal footing with the rich and the commoners rubbed shoulders with the notables. The chiefs, encountering Larcher for the first time, watched him closely. They had wrapped their heads in dark-blue turban cloth recently bought by the yard at the market. The carbon-paper-colored indigo dye imparted long bluish streaks to their hair and skin. A mixture of strong odors emanated from the group—a curious blend of cheap perfume, the aroma of incense, and the sweat of bodies.

When he came to Salah's son, Larcher greeted him with the ritual phrases. Ahmed was a young man of twenty-five, slightly built, with fine bones, and gentle eyes.

"My father received your kind invitation but was too fatigued to attend. He therefore asked that I present his salutations."

'You're welcome," said Larcher. "Please convey my greetings and best wishes for your father's recovery."

Ahmed was relieved that the officer had not rebuked him for his father's noticeable absence. Ahmed understood that Larcher had shown a respectable degree of courtesy and common politeness in keeping with conventions.

After making the rounds of the notables, Larcher himself sat down on the rugs. The kettles of water that had been singing on braziers in the patio were brought in and set before the tea-makers, who placed octagonal-shaped glasses on huge brass platters for the ceremonial tea-drinking. There were customary interruptions in conversation as the tray was passed. Out of respect for authority, the first glass of tea was drunk in silence. But gradually, in first one group and then another, tongues started to loosen while all anticipated the speeches to come. Larcher, capitalizing upon his influence, was in no hurry. While the second glass of tea was passed around he felt not the slightest pang of impatience as he conversed with his neighbors. When the third glass arrived, though, he decided it was time. He stood up and raised his hand to attract the attention of his listeners.

"I am glad that you all accepted my invitation. I arrived at Tindouf only a few months ago, and, because the region is so vast, this meeting became necessary. I felt that there should be no further delay in our getting to know each other. As you all know, at the upcoming fair we will have camel racing—long, medium, and short distance. All the entrants will be rewarded, with the winner receiving a racing camel and the others a sack of flour and sugar. Merchants from Colomb-Béchar and Goulimine will be at the fair in large numbers, so that you'll be able to sell your camels freely and stock up on provisions for the year. Finally, if you have any differences to settle, we are at your disposal. What we administrators are trying to do is maintain peace and concord among all of you. We have no other purpose. May the Lord help us and help you in this task. May He give you an abundance of rain for your pastures, may the sale of your camels go smoothly, may He give you salvation, peace and His mercy."

A murmur of approval ran through the gathering, which

warmly welcomed this humble speech. For the first time a district officer had avoided stern warnings couched in a patronizing tone. The approach was novel and impressed these men, who had a heightened awareness of the inflections inherent in their language.

Ghit ould Bouaha spoke for the Sellam after being prompted by Hamoudi, the residing chief. Hamoudi had chosen to remain silent because of the significant absence of Salah, his equal. Ghit, who might have been a painter's model of Christ with his pronounced features and full beard that merged into a shock of hair, seemed accustomed to this sort of exercise. In a thundering voice he began:

"May the Lord bless your parents and the parents of your parents, Commander, and may He make their final resting place to be in Paradise. We thank you for the words of peace from your mouth. They are good words which go to our hearts. The idea of organizing such an assembly is wise and generous. It combines usefulness with pleasure. It makes it possible to know our leaders—may Allah help them in their task, for, as the proverb goes, 'Knowledge of men is a treasure.' Of course, we of the Sellam know that we can count on you; you help the poor man when he is in trouble and the petitioner seeking his rights. You represent justice for us in our time of need by preserving peace and security. But you must know that the Sellam are devoted to you and are your loyal subjects. They have always paid their taxes, have always shown great hospitality to your representatives, and have always attended your meetings. The Sellam are not gossip-mongers who spread false rumors. They are an honest people who desire to live in peace and harmony with their neighbors and other tribes. May the peace of Allah be on you and on this assembly gathered today."

After this pledge of loyalty, the other sect felt obliged to respond. Hassan ould Bouali, the young chief of the Belgacem ou Brahim, directed a glance at Salah's son before making his intended reply. Unlike Ghit, who was a somewhat muddled speaker, Hassan had the air of an elegant speaker. He was noted for his neatly trimmed beard and carefully placed turban. His voice had none of the ring of the other man's but he looked as if he would make a formidable negotiator. The allusion to Salah's absence had been too clear to allow it to pass without mention. He came round to it skillfully.

"I share the words of my comrade Ghit in expressing to you, Commander, our gratitude for your warm invitation and kind words. May the Lord lengthen your days and the days of your comrades. May He help you in your uneasy task with such a turbulent people."

The crowd began to laugh. He continued:

"France knows the Reguibat. Despite their faults, they are an honorable people. You may count on them all without distinction as to class and tribe. We are one people even if we do sometimes feud. Do brothers of a family not sometimes quarrel among themselves? Although it may happen, the family always stays together. It is the same with us. Since your representatives arrived here we have not had cause to complain about the French. There have been times, it is true, when we were opposed to you, but these resentments have subsided. No serious problems will ever arise, so long as the administration respects us for our religion, customs, and Islamic Law. If your people sustain this prevailing attitude, then I can guarantee the full cooperation, not only of the Belgacem ou Brahim but also of my true brothers, the Legouacem. We must all coexist on the same earth, living in harmony and depending on Allah to decide our actions. May peace be unto you and this assembly."

It was obvious that Ghit had been unable to solve the feuding between tribes. Hassan had spoken as the leader of the Confederation, informing the administration that there would be certain limitations. The message seemed clear: Salah was not there because one condition had not been fulfilled. But which one? Religion—the authorities had never interfered; custom—everything had been done to respect it.

"I really don't see where we could have gone wrong,"

Larcher commented to his officers at the end of the meeting.

"It's clear enough," replied de Vignandeau, who after two years with the camel corps had a fair understanding of the problems. "The nomads have accused France of upsetting their traditional society with our democratic procedures. In a certain sense they're not altogether wrong. By attempting to establish equality, we have generated a situation in which the lowliest tribes have begun to take liberties with those of noble stature. Some are cooperative with respect to the administration but others are nursing a dangerous feeling of frustration and injustice. We are sitting on a keg of dynamite that is about to explode and I don't see any way to defuse it."

CHAPTER IV

The airplane carrying General Pignon lifted off the end of
the runway. It was an old three-engine Junker whose wings,
too big for the narrow fuselage, seemed to flap awkwardly like
those of some enormous bird. This departure ended the official
ceremonies at Choufane which had lasted three entire days.
For the duration of his stay, the general had reviewed a parade
of the camel corps, attended the camel races, and presided at a
sumptuous feast of twenty roasted sheep. Lastly, he had joined
in the highlight of the festivities—a southern Moroccan dance
known as the Guedra performed by Selma, a woman from
Goulimine. While Selma moved round and round, driven by

Dance known as the Guedra performed by Selma from Goulimine.

the guttural chanting of four Arab soldiers who clapped their hands rhythmically above her head, a single drum struck with slender olive-wood sticks served as accompaniment. She then kneeled, twisting her body gracefully, swinging long braids of hair that were richly ornamented with shells, beads of amber, and tiny spice vials. Still on her knees, she gestured with her fingers, arms, and body, in mimicry of a love dance. Two spotlights, piercing the darkness of night, illuminated the dancer and the players against a backdrop of multicolored rugs that had been hung from a tennis wall.

Aside from these folk festivities, General Pignon's spirit was appreciably influenced by the prevailing optimism of the fort. Because of the mutual trust he maintained with his troops, Larcher would be an excellent commander. His young lieutenants made a good team. They were unprejudiced men, dedicated to their profession and committed to doing their job without any serious illusions about the future. By comparison, their colleagues from southern Morocco, Marrakesh, and Agadir who had come expressly for the fair, had seemed out of step with reality. Did they clearly understand the coming danger? Morocco was predictably moving toward imminent independence. And yet these other officers plainly evidenced an overbearing confidence, a basic flaw that saddened Pignon. Reports had filtered in about the inception of a Moroccan liberation army and subversive bands now occupying the Drâa. But, to Pignon's great despair, none of the officers from Morocco had seemed to heed the warning. As the plane bound for Colomb-Béchar circled for the last time over the insignificant sand fort of Tindouf, Pignon felt that its semblance of tranquility would soon be shattered. The small oasis, with its haphazard boundaries, along the crossroads of different ethnic groups, faced an uncertain future. It might one day be caught between two conflicting currents of independence, to be crushed in their pincer-like grip.

While these ruminations ran through Pignon's mind, Larcher,

on the ground, was pocketing a telegram he had just received from the radio operator. Before directing his jeep back to the base, he summoned his officers for important news. A few moments later he read aloud the message which had put him in such good humor.

"District Officer at Ain Ben Tili to the Commanding Officer at Tindouf. This day, at 1500 hours, Mahmoud, son of Salah ould Ahmed, took refuge in the post and surrendered his rifle. Stop. He claims to have killed Mohammed ould Souilem of the tribe of the Sellam at Bir Lefjah. Stop. Request instructions."

Not one of the officers moved a muscle. Larcher, looking up over his glasses, threw an amused smile in their direction.

"I'm waiting for your reactions. You, de La Renaudie, what do you think?" Larcher liked de La Renaudie's keen analytical mind.

"It's a nasty business, sir; a severe blow to the prestige of Salah ould Ahmed and the Sidi Allal as a whole. The Sellam may use the incident to their advantage. It is a certainty that their chief, this old fox Hamoudi ould Himdoun, will act true to character."

Larcher showed surprise.

"I don't follow you—I'm not thinking of the Sellam. You're probably right, but the concerns of France are our top priority. For five years Salah ould Ahmed has refused to recognize French authority and now his son needs our refuge for protection. What a blow for the old man! Don't you think that we should take advantage of this? It's a heaven-sent opportunity."

Blizzard broke in.

"But sir, it'll be a great nuisance having a 'prince's son' for a prisoner."

"No, not at all. He's a prisoner who must be well treated although he has confessed to a murder on French soil."

Many of the officers smiled. They knew full well that this "French soil" was not even a measurable quantity.

"Well," Larcher resumed, "at least it is under French administrative control. So unless there are extenuating circumstances, we have to try the son and possibly sentence him. And in point of fact why did he do it? Any ideas, Vogel?"

"I don't have much experience in these things. A crime of passion? The Reguibat know all about love but I don't think you'll find them killing for a woman. Far from it."

There was a chuckle from the officers.

"It's more likely, I think, to be a dispute over water rights. Bir Lefjah belongs to the Sellam, and Mahmoud must have taken his camel to drink there. Although he's entitled to do so according to custom, the others may have made rude remarks or fired over his head. Who knows? I expect it's the usual sort of thing but it's taken on more importance because it involves both the Sellam and the Sidi Allal—as well as the son of the most important man among them."

De Vignandeau, the most experienced officer of the camel corps, spoke up.

"I agree with Vogel. It's probably the kind of ordinary event that happens all the time. The great nomad tribes don't quarrel over pastureland the way people do in other parts of the world because the areas are so vast. But when it comes to watering places there are constant disputes over ownership and use. As for the trial, sir, how do you propose to go about it? Under French laws?"

"Yes. Most likely at the nearest criminal court in Columb-Béchar."

The reaction of the officers was unanimous.

"But that's ludicrous," de La Renaudie burst out. "We should try him under the customary laws of the Reguibat, at a great gathering of the Sidi Allal and the Sellam. We will be in the role of benevolent observers. The price of blood will be paid by the criminal's family and Salah will lose face in our presence."

"You're not with me, gentlemen," said Larcher, his temper beginning to rise. "You don't understand anything. You're caught up so much in the nomad mentality that you're beginning to think like the Reguibat. First, I don't want Salah to lose face, as you say, in front of us. It would be a point against us. Moreover, I know it's ridiculous to take a 'French citizen' like this young man, drive him over 600 miles from here to Colomb-Béchar, and demand his appearance before a criminal court. But think a moment. Salah will no longer be able to say that he doesn't recognize France. He will be forced to deal with us. At least I hope so."

"This will apply only if he loves his son," interrupted Vogel. "However, these men have so many children that it is uncertain if he will fight to save him. In this instance I feel that, since Mahmoud is the last-born son, Salah will acquiesce to our wishes. Mahmoud is a twenty-year-old boy from the second marriage, an unusual occurrence among the monogamous nomads. It's a good bet that Mahmoud is a favorite son and that Salah will take some risks for him."

"In other words," de La Renaudie broke in sarcastically, "there's a red burnoose in the offing."

The men burst into hearty laughter.

"Why not?" replied Larcher. "I don't know how else to bring him around. Since we have his son, he will be the one coming to see me."

"I call that blackmail, his son for a cloak," replied de La Renaudie.

Larcher went purple in the face.

"Call it what you like. The important thing is to preserve appearances and to regain our credibility with this business. We didn't start it, it occurred by chance. But if we were to act in any other way, we'd be the laughing-stock of the Reguibat. 'Look,' they'd say, 'the commander had a chance to catch the old man Salah and he let it slip by.' No. In politics there is no blackmail. Or phrased differently, blackmail is a constant. In this case, the circumstances have set the scenario for black-mail, even if we were to pretend it did not exist."

"We've been lucky, that's all," Vogel added. "But that doesn't guarantee the acceptance of the cloak by Salah."

"If forced to don the cloak," Blizzard pointed out, "Salah would become our erstwhile enemy. Salah associates the cloak with humiliation. This would impel him towards Morocco with all his arms and belongings."

"A fat lot of good that would do him," exclaimed de Vignandeau. "What a present to His Moroccan Majesty."

The talk had gone on long enough, thought Larcher. He was becoming impatient. He hated this kind of chitchat, which he referred to as "cafe-talk." He directed the conversation to a more productive result.

"When will the news reach here?"

"Bir Lefjah," Vogel explained, pointing with his finger on a map, "is four days' camel ride by forced march from Tindouf. One of the Sellam has already left for Bir Lefjah to warn the Sheikh. So the news will surface in three days at the earliest."

"Good," Larcher said. "Ahmed, Salah's eldest son, and the principal nobles of the Sidi Allal and Belgacem ou Brahim will have to leave the village before then. I don't want any vengeance along the lines of Talion Law. The Sellam, in their confusion, might do something regrettable. De La Renaudie, take your men out at first light tomorrow and confiscate all the nomads' weapons. Tell them you have to verify the serial numbers. Then you can give them back a few at a time. Get the Sidi Allal and the Belgacem ou Brahim moving first. Then a couple of days later you can approach the Sellam."

"Yes, sir."

"Blizzard and de Vignandeau, you go to Sheikh Mantallah ould Senhouri, the acting mayor of the village. Have dinner with him and at the end of the meal tell him quietly what's happened. I think we can count on his discretion. Because Salah will have nothing but scorn for this mayor who belongs to the Tajakant tribe, the mayor may reciprocate by aiding us in this task. And as he will want to maintain peace in the village, he will help us collect the weapons.

"Vogel, take two vehicles bound for Ain Ben Tili and bring

Mahmoud back. Try to question him to learn all the details of this business. But go easy on him."

"I'll leave this evening," Vogel answered, "but with just six-by-six Dodge jeep. I'll get Master Sergeant Laurent, who is a fine mechanic, to be my driver. A second vehicle would only delay us. We'll take along some spare parts—water pump, carburetor, contact points, Delco distributor, a set of springs, an extra spare, and a fifty-gallon drum of gas. Plus two native soldiers and a guide, Brahim ould Kountaoui."

"Yes, your preparations are commendable. Although the track is marked, you may lose it. Anything is possible in this desert territory."

"It just occurred to me that we could go by way of Salah ould Ahmed's encampment. It's sixty-odd miles north of Ain Ben Tili. If I'm going to travel for two hundred miles, I can just as easily go the extra sixty. It'll give me a chance to see him and give him firsthand knowledge of what's happened. It's advisable that we also put him on his guard against any possible action by the Sellam and observe his reactions. I can accomplish my purpose without humiliating him or degrading our stature. We have an honorable pretext for the visit and he will be obligated to us."

Larcher gave him a look that was part astonishment, part admiration. The "young pup" was showing signs of promise.

"That's an excellent suggestion. But on your way back with Mahmoud, there must be no question of taking the time to bring him to his father."

"I won't take the risk, and besides, I'll have to make my way back with due haste."

CHAPTER V

Salah, who had been lying on a bare mat, sat up, and with a sudden movement removed the *chéche* covering his face. He mopped the beads of sweat on his brow, swearing at the buzzing flies that had settled on his face and arms. He cursed the household servants for placing his tent too close to the animal corral, a foul-smelling enclosure that attracted insects. He was engaged in a continual battle against the bad habits of lazy camel herders, and he made a mental note to lecture them during the evening's tea service after the animals had been taken care of. Acting upon the day's accounts, Salah would distribute compliments, criticism, and punishment.

He was in a bad temper. He had indigestion from the midday

meal of smoke-cured meat steeped in melted butter, a dish he could not resist. He cast a critical eye at the shadow of the tent post outside. Its fullness told him clearly that the hours for prayer were past. Old Abdallah, *muezzin* for the camp, must still be sleeping. But Salah wanted his tea first. It was that blessed time of the day when the air began to stir gently, hinting at the freshness to come as the sun began its descent over the scorched horizon, where a dry haze still lingered. The piping-hot beverage was a satisfying remedy for parched throats.

Salah emitted a roar. The small slave who had been sleeping in the back of the tent, mouth wide open and unconscious of the flies that gathered about his lips, bounded to his feet and ran to the kettle on the cold embers outside. In his haste to serve his master, he caught his feet in the tent ropes, falling headlong but afterwards righting himself, only to spill part of the water he had taken from a goatskin. He managed, however, to speak with formal politeness.

"It is ready, lord, it will be ready in a minute from now, as you command, lord."

At that precise moment a young herder was seen running as fast as his legs could carry him, his garment, belted at the waist, billowing with the onrushing air as he raced along. He hurtled down the nearby hill and headed straight for Salah's tent. Salah stiffened in expectation of some extraordinary news. Breathlessly, the herder spoke.

"A vehicle is approaching. I could see the dust it raised."

"One or two?"

"Just one, my lord."

Salah wondered for a moment. It was not unusual at this hour, when it was still very hot, for herders to be prey to hallucinations and mirages. Spontaneous eddies of warm air—which popular tradition attributed to local spirits—were common in these parts. They were sometimes so strong and moved so swiftly along the ground at just the right height in a motionless sky as to seem like a cloud of dust. Besides, the camp was not near a road. Any approaching motor vehicle would have to be adapted for every kind of terrain and thus could only be army issue. And such vehicles never traveled alone, for obvious security reasons.

With an instinctive response innate to nomads, Salah knelt down, and placed his ear to the sand. The sound of a motor, faint at first but gradually becoming stronger, could be heard. He held his breath as he had a sudden premonition. A bearer of bad news was approaching. For five years he had avoided having anything to do with the French administration. And they had never made an effort to meet him. Was he going to be arrested? He didn't think it very likely, not with such a small unit.

He didn't pursue this line of thought for long. A Dodge six-by-six appeared on the outskirts of the camp, slowed down, and came to a halt. Salah noted this, and was appreciative. He issued orders, summoned the heads of the nearby tents, and asked his wife Meriem, through the curtain that separated the women's quarters from the men's, to pass him a clean *chéche* and robe. He changed, smoothed down his hair with the palm of his hand, and stroked his beard in a familiar gesture. He was ready. His men arrived, still groggy and not fully awake.

"What are they doing?" Salah asked one of his advisors.

"Nothing for the moment. They're getting out of the vehicle."

"How many are there?"

"Not many. Two natives, a driver, an officer, and a guide."

"In any case they are respecting the rules of politeness by avoiding the center of the encampment. Abdallah, go to meet with them. Then bring them back here and say the customary words. The rest of you spread out the rugs, have the kettles put on the braziers, and look a bit more alive. Go and tell your women to keep the children in the tents."

Salah breathed deeply, glad to show that he was still leader and that he knew how to retain his composure and command.

"Are they armed? I can't see very well from here."

"The natives have rifles. Can't tell about the driver. The officer is not armed."

Abdallah went off, limping on the right leg that had never healed after his awkward fall from a camel. The sound of his stentorian welcome could already be heard. The officer and guide replied. They were the only two to come forward. Salah did some quick thinking. This was evidently a visit of a peaceful nature. Perhaps the patrol had gotten lost and the officer was seeking help or information. But there was a dull feeling nagging at his heart. Salah continued to give his orders:

"When the lieutenant reaches the first tent, about the middle of the camp, you will go forward to greet him. Bring him to me. When you are ten yards from my tent, I shall come out for the welcoming. Understand?"

"We understand, my lord."

Everything moved very quickly from that point on just as Salah had planned. With a fixed smile on his lips, he carefully enunciated the ritual words of welcome, beginning with the most beautiful which the Prophet Mohammed had reserved for Ali when he came to request the hand of his daughter.

"*Ahlan wa sahlan wa marhaban bikoum.* Welcome to my family. Enter. My tent is your tent."

"May Allah increase your well-being and ours," Lieutenant Vogel replied.

The small group sat down cross-legged, eyes fixed on the rug, to initiate the formal ceremony of politeness.

"Welcome, welcome, there is not ill with you?"

While he intoned the ritual words of welcome, Salah studied his visitors. The lieutenant had an honest face; he was young, and his blue *kepi*, though covered with brownish dust from the journey, revealed in places the newness of its velour. Tall and slim, he made a good appearance. His Arabic, though still

The French officer in the nomadic tent. "A camel rider"

hesitant, was correct—as was his pronunciation. He seemed to be at ease and to know the customs. He bore with apparent stoicism the flies, the heat, and the scalding hot tea that he drank in little sips in the proper manner. His guide, a tall, gaunt man with a pointed beard, probably belonged to one of those tribes on the border between the sedentaries and the nomads, known as the Kounta or Tajakant, for whom Salah had nothing but contempt. But tribal considerations apart, the man, whose name was Hamdi, seemed rather friendly and displayed an air of false indolence and humility, signs of a good education.

Vogel was formulating his own observations. Salah's naturally stiff bearing kept his back very straight and gave his figure a particularly imposing appearance. He was not a tall man and his double chin hinted at a certain portliness. His nose was very straight, slightly aquiline, and led down to a narrow mouth scarcely made for smiling. A wide, slightly rounded forehead was surmounted by a straight fringe of hair somewhat in the style common in Flemish paintings. His small eyes were lively and very light blue, with a direct look. Vogel was struck with the whiteness of his skin, the slenderness of his ankles and wrists, and the elegance of his long, manicured hands that clearly saw no manual work.

The second glass of tea was served, more heavily sugared than the first. It was time now for the master of ceremonies to proceed from conventional politeness to general topics, such as the weather, by which the visitor's identity and purpose might be ascertained.

"Was the road good?"

"Very good. We left Tindouf yesterday in the late afternoon."

"You made good progress. Allah be praised. Traveling alone, you didn't fear a breakdown?"

"No, we have a mechanic with us and the vehicle is in good condition. We were also in a hurry."

Salah did not dare to ask why. He thought that by the third

glass of tea some further clarifications would probably emerge. He nonetheless asked about the *choufan*.

"I deeply regret that my state of health did not permit my acceptance of the kind invitation of the authorities to go to the *choufan*. I delegated my eldest son, Ahmed, to go. I trust he behaved himself."

"Everything went very well, and the camel market is still going strong."

Vogel made a sign to the guide, who came out with a torrent of information on the prices paid at the market and the events that had taken place. His language was both precise and pompous, rather as if he were reciting a great epic. Salah and his companions attentively listened to determine the actual truth and the significance of the visit from the various intonations in his voice.

"They rode camels in good condition, including she-camels, milk camels, and young—all of them sound. There were black and white sheep with much wool and fine goats that could hardly walk from being so fat. One bale of wool sold for eighty dourous—truly a great price. There was an abundance of camel hair, of black goat hair, of cushions and saddles for men and women, mats in goat hair, beautiful sheepskins."

"God be praised. How much for a first-class racing camel, the most expensive?"

"For the most expensive 15,000 dourous, and the least expensive was an animal eighteen months old that sold for 1,500."

"And the sheep?"

"The dearest ones for 1,300 and kids for 400; lambs sold for 250 to 300. There were great quantities of merchandise. Allah be praised. Merchants and buyers flocked to the market from all around and from every country."

"Did you take part in the great race?"

"Yes, of course. A camel of the Sellam won, and two of the Foqra of Hadj Said won in the endurance race. In the speed race it was the son of Bouhali of the Sidi Allal and one of the Oulad Sid Ahmed who were the winners."

"Who were those who made the most profit?"

"The Sidi Allal on camels and the Ahal Zeribir on sheep. All the animals led to market were sold."

"And the competition of skill?"

"It was Mahmoud ould Benane who won."

"Allah be praised. It must be as He wants."

Eventually Vogel realized that an hour had passed. It was time, now after they had finished the third glass of tea, to move on to action. He didn't quite know how to start. As the bearer of secret news, he wanted to tell the old chief privately so as to spare his feelings. He addressed Salah:

"I would like to speak with you alone."

"That need present no difficulty."

Salah waved his hand. All the men rose and promptly left the tent. The moment of truth had arrived. Salah, to conceal his nervousness, took beads out of the embroidered pocket of his robe and began to intone the name of Allah as each bead of amber passed through his fingers on the fine cord. Vogel removed his *kepi*, mopped his brow, and made an effort to speak in classical Arabic to give greater solemnity to his words:

"May it please Allah. I am instructed by my superiors to announce important news only to you."

"May it please Allah," replied Salah, his face tense with emotion.

"Your son, Mahmoud, has killed a Sellam, Mohammed ould Souilem, at Bir Lefjah. He was pursued and sought refuge at the post at Ain Ben Tili, placing himself under the protection of France. I have been ordered to take him to Tindouf. Knowing that your encampment was not far from the route of my journey, I came here to tell you the news on the order of my superior and in deference to you. The news has been kept secret at Tindouf to avoid any incident between the tribes that are still there. But I wanted you to be warned so that you might take such steps as you think necessary."

Salah did not flinch. Only his fingers moved the beads more quickly and a slight tremor ran through his shoulders, but otherwise his head remained high and motionless. A long silence ensued between the two men, who stared at each other steadily. With an assurance Vogel admired, Salah finally spoke:

"If my son killed, it is because he was forced to. He exercised his legitimate right to self-defense."

"How can you say that, since you don't know the circumstances surrounding the tragedy?"

"I do not know the incident but I know my son. He is loyal, pure, and noble. If he killed, it is because he was provoked by those Sellam dogs. And that is the fault of France."

"How so?"

"Because you have given equal rights to servants and masters. The Sellam were our inferiors and you put them on an equal footing with us, a grave mistake on the part of the administration. Let each stay in his place according to our customs and Moslem law. You have sown trouble in people's minds. You reap the harvest of tragedy."

"Your language belongs to another century. All men are equal and you are the leader of the entire confederation of the Legouacem."

"Yes, but because of your aberrant policy small men raise their heads. They no longer obey and they undermine our authority. What do you plan to do with Mahmoud?"

"Question him first, then try him."

"How can you try him? It is for the assembly of the Reguibat to try him and determine the price of blood. What is France's role in any of this?"

"France administers the country and protects you. The best proof is that your son, being in danger, took refuge under France's benign influence. France therefore applies her law insofar as she is concerned. Now, in the present instance,

France is involved since this concerns a serious incident between two tribes for which she is responsible. Customary law, of course, is something else. It is for you to decide what you must do. This does not concern us. We do not want to be involved in that aspect."

Salah suddenly felt that he had gone too far. Now that the initial shock had passed, grief began to creep upon him. His breathing was heavy. His son, Mahmoud, his youngest son, in French jails! A rush of anger, quickly suppressed, shook him. Why had the boy not taken refuge in the camp among his own? Had there perhaps not been time or had he not wanted to create problems for his father? Would the French hold him prisoner for long? To break the silence which had taken hold, Vogel added:

"You can count on us to take care of Mahmoud. He will not be mishandled or badly treated."

"Thank you. We are all in the hands of Allah. It is He who decides."

The two men rose, and Salah left the tent to accompany his visitor, walking in measured steps, majestic in his stiff robe. Knowing that they could be heard, they carefully acted out the words of farewell: "Truly you will not stay? We would be glad. The tent for our guests is in place. We would sacrifice a camel for you."

"May Allah increase your well-being and ours. Thank you for your hospitality. But we are pressed for time and important tasks await us."

"May God help you and protect you. Till our next meeting."

CHAPTER VI

The fort at Ain Ben Tili, a square, featureless building, was situated in the middle of an immense sparsely vegetated plain. It looked as if it were a pâpier-maché set left on the stage of some deserted theater. Its walls could be seen for miles and to a person approaching by camel they appeared to continually recede.

This was not the case today as Vogel's six-by-six quickly sped past the archway. It stopped by the small fountain—situated in the middle of the court but totally bereft of water. Chief Adjutant Durand, commanding officer at the fort, came forward and saluted. He looked pleased.

"I'm glad to see you. You made good time. Did you come for Mahmoud?"

"Yes, that's why I'm here."

"He's not difficult and he has given me no trouble. But I'm worried that the Sellam, knowing he's here, might decide to attack the post."

"We are well aware of this contingency. That's why we wanted to quickly escort him to safety at Tindouf. Where is he?"

"There, to the right of the archway."

Vogel went immediately towards a young man of medium build who was squatting with his back against the wall. His face showed regular features, framed by smooth, dark hair. His big black eyes showed a wild expression—the look of a hunted animal evading his pursuers. Mahmoud rose when he saw the officer, but Vogel motioned that he return to his position and sat down himself on the ground, cross-legged.

"Peace and prosperity be with you," he began. "You are now under France's protection. You may speak without fear. Tell me what happened."

"May there be only peace and goodness," replied Mahmoud. And in a voice that was hesitant at first but gradually gaining in confidence, he began to tell his story in detail.

When Mahmoud stopped speaking, Vogel reflected a moment. It had been three days since the murder. The Sellam would have buried the dead man by now and perhaps had separated into two groups, one heading for Tindouf to alert their chief, the other following Mahmoud's trail. But they probably had not thought of using the trail that led to Ain Ben Tili. They would never expect that Salah ould Ahmed's son would take refuge there. On the other hand, they might have decided to stage a punitive raid against Salah's camp. However, Salah had been informed, and had no doubt already moved his camp and taken other measures to protect himself. So it didn't seem as if the present predicament would worsen immediately.

"You admit having killed Mohammed ould Souilem?"

"Yes," replied Mahmoud. "But I had no other choice. Would you listen to insults against your father if you were armed and if you were despised so much that your warnings weren't taken seriously? I was threatened by these men and I had a legitimate right to clear myself, my family, and the entire Sidi Allal of any dishonor."

"I must arrest you for deliberate homicide, a matter which will be decided by French judicial procedures. You will be given the opportunity to appear before a magistrate with a duly appointed attorney. In your defense you may plead your cause of honor, during which time no harm will be inflicted upon your person. Do I have your word that you will not attempt an escape? So I shall regard you as just another traveling companion sharing our journey of life?"

"Since I came here to ask for your protection, you have my word. Do what you will with me. I am in your hands and Allah's. May His will be done."

Vogel decided to begin his return trip from Ain Ben Tili that evening. He advised Durand to keep his men on the alert and to post sentinels in and around the fort even though any sign of danger appeared to have subsided.

With their vehicle back on the road again Mahmoud conversed with the two Arab soldiers who sat on either side of him. It didn't serve any purpose, thought Vogel, to bind and humiliate him. He would not try to escape. The road had been good so far; later it would become hard and characteristically like corrugated iron. They would have to accelerate on that stretch so as to minimize the bumpiness, although this would undoubtedly cause passenger discomfort and wreck the suspension.

The ground was still soft and Laurent took advantage of it to drive fast, often raising a magnificent cloud of yellowish dust behind him.

Suddenly a family of antelope appeared on the crest of a low nearby hill. The male was distinguished by his twisted horns, while the female sported smooth antlers, and those of the young were barely visible. The male took a few steps and then stood stock still, facing the danger that he vaguely sensed, while the mother and her young darted away at top speed. Thus the father, the sacrificial victim, stood motionless, in order to save his own. Yielding to the urging of his companions, Vogel allowed the vehicle to stop. To prevent a wild flurry of bullets, he permitted only one of the natives to fire. Brahim ould Kountaoui took steady aim from the running-board. The target, one hundred yards away and illuminated by the rays of the sinking sun, was clearly visible. The bullet fell three feet short of the animal. He turned and sped off on his graceful legs. Vogel hesitated, but there was such excitement among the men that he let them take up the pursuit, not without some misgivings. Brahim, balanced on the running-board and braced against the spare wheel, fired at more or less regular intervals without success. The antelope began to show signs of fatigue but it still kept running. Tired of the chase, Vogel took Brahim's place, intent on finishing the hunt as quickly as possible. At the precise moment he took the gun the animal swung off at a right angle and moved far ahead of the vehicle. It was too late to take aim. Vogel fired instinctively in much the same manner as peasants in Touraine on the first day of pheasant hunting. The antelope took the bullet full in the shoulder, spun round in the air, and crashed downward, its shoulder blade dislocated. Brahim raced toward it, knife in hand, shouting: "It's still alive!" That was important because only game killed in accordance with Moslem law could be eaten. It was essential to pretend that the antelope, brought down by an unbeliever, still clung to life until sacrificed by a Moslem. Brahim grasped the animal firmly, turned its head towards Mecca, and ran the blade of his dagger in an arc across its throat. He slit the jugular artery, just below the jaw. As he did so, he exclaimed, "In the name of Allah the Merciful, Allah the Compassionate."

The sun was almost down and it was decided to spend the

night there. There was still enough light to collect wood to build a fire. Everybody, regardless of rank, quickly lent a hand. When the wood was collected Vogel sat down on a sheepskin, waiting till the tea was made and poured into glasses. He invited Mahmoud to sit down next to him. In this atmosphere of relaxation, the conversation turned to various subjects. Mahmoud had a great admiration for his father.

"I want to thank you for having warned him. He must have already broken camp by now."

So Mahmoud had already been informed. It was only to be expected that the natives would have told him.

"Where do you suppose he is headed?" asked Vogel.

"To the north, of course, with the intention of joining Moulay Mehdi's camp. There will be safety there. How did my father take the news?"

"Your father has great confidence in you. He assumed that you had killed legitimately in self-defense."

Mahmoud, satisfied, added with an understanding air:

"My father knows me."

"And your mother? How do you think she reacted?"

"My mother died when I was four years old. I hardly knew her. The woman who has been mother to me is Salah's wife, Meriem, whom I adore and who brought me up. She must be weeping at this moment."

"Did your mother belong to the Brahim ou Daoud?"

"Yes, she was a niece to Moulay Mehdi, and Meriem is the daughter of Moulay Mehdi."

"Has your father had other wives?"

"No, only two. Meriem, his present wife, who's been married to him for thirty years, and Salambouha, who brought me into the world and who died after only five years of marriage."

Mahmoud was talking more easily now while they were drinking tea. He discussed the relations he had with his half-brothers, stepmother, and father. He had been the only child of Salah's second marriage. He described Salambouha's premature death. Vogel did not venture to go further in his inquiry this first day. The main thing was for Mahmoud to feel he could trust the officer. From this conversation Vogel drew the impression that Salah ould Ahmed's family was a close one.

The first pieces of the antelope were brought over. They consisted of flame-sizzled liver, which Vogel shared with Mahmoud while waiting for the noodles and tomato sauce— the staple of the *mehariste*. They all began to feel the coldness of the night air, but the fine and tender flesh of the antelope induced a sort of infectious well-being among the little group in the desert. The meal finished, the men lay down on the ground, wrapped in their blankets. Vogel contemplated the stars before falling asleep; the constellations shone brilliantly in the crisp, dry atmosphere. He thought of his comrades sleeping in barracks and bivouacs and considered himself fortunate. The purity of the sky was magic to him.

CHAPTER VII

As soon as the French patrol had left, Salah ould Ahmed decided to break camp. He announced his decision to the tribal members at that evening's convocation. After taking several deep draughts of the day's fresh milk, customarily passed around in a wooden *calabash*, his voice broke the silence.

"O men, the hour is serious. Mahmoud, my son and yours, has been attacked by the Sellam. He defended himself and in his doing so has killed Mohammed ould Souilem at the well of Bir Lefjah. He has since placed himself under the protection of the authorities at Ain Ben Tili.

"You know the Sellam. They are a most violent and vindictive people. We must assume that they will seek retribution against us and our possessions. I would like each of you to be on his guard. Tomorrow, immediately after the first prayers at dawn we will break camp and head farther north. We will approach the encampment of our brother Moulay Mehdi, our ally of the Belgacem ou Brahim and a member of the Brahim ou Daoud.

"We are limited in number and our young men have not yet returned from *choufan* at Tindouf. As a further complication, we only have four guns. Those with arms will escort the caravan: two on each side, one in front and one in the rear. Since there is no time to dawdle along on foot, it will be necessary that all the men and women ride. Pregnant women, mothers with infants, and newborn goats will be placed in litters. Our tents will not be erected but will remain folded for the duration of the journey. Since the weather is good we will sleep under the stars. We will stop for water only once, and in five days we should reach our destination."

The question of the herds was more difficult since the animals had to be sorted out. Old animals and she-camels with foals under six months of age, which would travel separately, had to be segregated from the gelded animals, stallions, and young animals. Different drivers were assigned the various tasks; routes were chosen according to the nature of the herds and the caravan's speed of travel. It was also agreed upon that, when the time came for departing, the caravan carrying the men, women, children, and baggage would circle the camp three times before heading north so as to blur its tracks. Some of the herd would cross the tracks of the caravan at precisely determined places—in the center of the *wadis*, for example. Scant precautions, thought Salah, for nomads were used to reading camel tracks with little difficulty. But these tracks might very well serve as a diversion, delaying possible pursuit and helping to gain time. It was important not to neglect anything. "We are weak," Salah said aloud, "so we must be cunning and use our wits."

As always, Salah impressed his listeners with the lucidity of his proposals and his decisive organization. He had calculated the exact details involved and efficiently assigned the various tasks. He rose and invited the gathering to pray as they did every evening, but this time with more seriousness than usual. Allah alone knew what tomorrow held for them! The thirty or so men ranged themselves in two lines behind Salah, who, as their *imam*, led the prayers. It was the dinner prayer, the fifth and last prayer of the day. In his strong voice Salah began with the invocation, "Allah is most great," which was repeated by the men, and then recited aloud the *Fatiha* or first *sura* of the Koran, the beginning of the Holy Book.

Later, alone in his tent after a difficult day charged with emotion, Salah lay down and called to his wife, Meriem, from behind the dividing curtain. As she sat down near him he stretched out and placed his head on her lap, a favorite position of relaxation. Meriem was weeping.

"If you keep on, you're going to make me cry," he told her.

"My poor Mahmoud, my son, in French prisons. I can only imagine how much he's going to suffer."

"You mustn't exaggerate. He's safe. Let us thank Allah for that! The French will not harm him. It's only a question of time. He will be returned to us safe and sound, Allah willing."

"Yes, but how very much we will miss him, this lively youth with his joy for living."

While she was speaking, Meriem gently ran her hand through Salah's hair, a habit she had picked up from rubbing a perfumed unguent made of camel marrow on his head as a remedy for hair loss. Salah was grateful to her for her affection and her supportive presence. As the daughter of Moulay Mehdi, Salah's cousin, she had been betrothed to Salah at an early age. He had always appreciated her kindness, even temper, and sense of duty. Like all young well-bred girls she had followed a strict milk regimen once she had attained a marriageable age. She would drink several quarts of milk a day for months on end under the strict supervision of her mother to achieve the desired bridal weight. Thus she had done honor to her family and the amount of her dowry in milk camels would be even higher. The custom was a good one, thought Salah. A plump woman was generally very wise, a good mother, and a source of freshness and comfort to her husband. However, Meriem's early fullness had further increased over the years. Salah had never been physically attracted to her, but nevertheless she had gained his respect by giving him four children, two daughters and two sons.

That evening he was unable to sleep and his mind wandered back into the past. He remembered the day when Meriem, in the course of just such an evening as this, had said in a gentle voice:

"Salah, you're still a young man of forty-five years, and although I am the same age, I feel like an old woman. My excessive weight prevents me from easily moving around and I find it increasingly difficult to perform my daily tasks."

"What does that mean?" he had replied. "Do you want me to buy another slave for you? Nothing could be simpler. Why didn't you say so before?"

"That's not the issue. I am well aided by oum Zeineb, our kindly black slave whom we've had for over twenty years and who capably takes care of the children. She is virtually a daughter to us. I was referring to something else."

"I don't see what."

"You see, you are in your prime whereas I am no longer able to give you children. I don't have the same desire I used to and I believe in all honesty that you should have a second wife."

"You shouldn't think that way. I am happy with you and I need nothing. The Prophet—may Allah grant him salvation and His blessings—allows us four legitimate wives. But you know that among us one wife is practically the rule."

Nevertheless, Meriem wouldn't budge from her idea and she returned to it several times. One day, tired of the battle, Salah said: "Listen, I'll accept your proposition, but with the condition that you choose the woman who is to be my new wife."

Meriem smiled in an odd sort of way. "This is exactly what I had intended to do, and the choice has been already decided upon. You will be agreeably surprised. The girl is young— twenty years younger than you. She's a niece of Moulay Mehdi and therefore a second cousin of mine. I'm sure she will please you."

Salah was to remember for the rest of his life the day his new bride arrived. When the camel bringing her crouched in the middle of the camp, his men fired their rifles into the air in celebration. Salambouha promptly jumped to the ground and unabashedly oved toward Meriem by Salah's side. The two cousins kissed while the other women who had come to watch gave their traditional shouts of joy. Salambouha then turned to Salah, staring at him with bold but not quite brazen eyes and remarked, "So here's the old man I'm intended for. He's not too bad for his age."

Salah and Meriem burst out laughing, charmed by the young woman's spontaneity and feigned insolence. Salah fell in love with her from that first moment. Salambouha was of the new generation and had refused to follow the milk regimen at marriageable age. As a result, she had remained slim and small-waisted with delicate features, and a small and slightly upturned nose and flashing eyes, constantly moving and laughing. She was the epitome of a coquette. The garments worn by nomad women—swathes of layered fabric—scarcely lent themselves to elegance. But Salambouha knew how to make the most of them, and by dint of a fold here and tuck there she had managed to give her supple, graceful figure sufficient shape to attract attention. Whenever she walked near him, moving her own distinctive way, Salah felt his heart leap. During the times that they were apart, he was immediately drawn back to her and experienced intense desire. She took pains with her appearance, especially her hair. Sometimes she would wear very thin braids—enlisting the help of her friends to plait them—and then the braids would swing to and fro as she moved her body. Other times she would choose a more sophisticated style and don a broad hair band encrusted with shells, coral, glass beads, and tiny sachets of aromatic spices.

She had sufficient imagination to bring an element of suspense to their meetings and a special flavor to their love-play. In the evening when she came to lie beside him, a wave of intense happiness would sweep over Salah. Her way of kissing and giving caresses would send him into rapture. She made love with such conviction and intensity that their bodies would be in perfect harmony and he felt as if he were melting in her like sugar into water. He nicknamed her "my little *fennec*," from the name of the little desert fox which she resembled with her darting eyes and slender limbs. In certain aspects of her character she also identified with this animal, such as in her unpredictability. She called Salah "my *azouzel*"—the name the Reguibat used for their racing camels—and she liked to make a pun of its plural by saying, "of all the *azouazil*, you are my *azouzel*." Sometimes she would come silently and throw herself pensively into his arms, snuggling against his shoulder. At other times she would sulk inexplicably or show anger over some trifle; she would pretend she didn't want him by resisting his advances. Then he would clasp her around the waist and she would struggle, hammering on his chest with her little fists and telling him with a wild look in her eyes, "You will not have my soul." In their own intimate language this meant that she would not respond to his kisses. Salah, playing the game, would release his grip, with a veil of sadness clouding his face. Suddenly assuaged, Salambouha would become very tender. Slowly she would bring her face close to his to end in a long passionate kiss until he gasped for breath. Then, in the midst of this dreamlike state, she would utter the final words: "You have not had my soul. I've had yours."

Salambouha's charm did not reside solely in her physical attractiveness. She was a woman of lively intelligence. Despite her youth, inexperience, and lowly stature in the social hierarchy, she had won the hearts of all the women in the camp. Surprisingly, they had shown her friendship instead of jealousy. She had rapidly become familiar with these other personalities, and through diplomacy had gained their affections. For one, Meriem adored her. The two women spent their days together, inviting each other to their respective quarters. Salambouha willingly helped Meriem in her daily tasks. In the afternoon she would gather the women around her and tell them amusing stories. She also had a fine voice and used to sing the songs of southern Morocco or the love songs of the wandering minstrels of Mauritania. Salah, whose religious office did not permit him to be present for this secular entertainment, used to invent various reasons for going near the tent to hear them. And at night when they were alone, he would ask her in a subdued tone to sing those songs close to his ear.

Salambouha was unlike the other women, and her religious education was relatively sophisticated. Her father had taught her to read and to recite whole passages of the Koran. This made Salah very proud. It had not taken him long to realize that she gave him excellent advice, expressing her opinions with a sense of humor without meddling in the affairs of men. He often consulted her for a clear, objective opinion before making an important decision.

At the end of the first year Salambouha had brought a son into the world, Mahmoud. Salah was the happiest of men and he never tired of thanking Meriem, whom he had not neglected, for he was a good Moslem. He conformed to the law and spent every other night with her despite his aching desire for Salambouha. Meriem, who was quite without jealousy, suggested that he disregard the rules and spend more time with Salambouha. But Salah knew that he must strictly abide by Moslem law and he scrupulously divided his time equally between both wives.

Five years passed in this happy state. It was a fruitful time for Salah. His herds multiplied, his authority over the entire confederation increased, and his relations with the administration improved. And then, suddenly everything collapsed. Allah's designs are unfathomable. As it is written in the Koran: "From Him we come and to Him we return." One morning Salambouha complained of a violent headache and was coughing. Salah thought she had caught a cold and he ordered hot compresses and cupping-glasses to be applied. Meriem never left her bedside and cared for her like a mother. But, despite all the remedies, her condition only worsened. She kept to her bed all day long, her body wracked by fever, her face drawn. In the late afternoon Salah would take her outside, urging her to walk a few steps. Pale and weak, she rested on his shoulder, content with his attentions. But the effort quickly exhausted her. On the sixth day she coughed up blood and lay prostrate on her couch, hardly moving the entire day. The following afternoon she summoned Salah and asked that she be taken out of the tent. Picking her up in his arms he walked slowly out onto the sand in the direction of the open desert. She had lost weight and was as light as a sparrow. He felt the heat of her body against his chest and now and then, when he bent his head to speak to her, he saw her sad eyes.

"My own *fennec*, my little fox, you're going to be better soon, I promise you."

She replied in a very tired voice:

"My own *azouzel*, if I should leave soon for a long, solitary journey, promise me you will watch over our son Mahmoud with all your heart."

Suddenly Salah felt her become heavy as when a child falls asleep in the arms of its father. Her arm, which she had placed around his neck, slid down his body and swung loosely as he walked. He hardly dared to realize what had happened. Talking incoherently, he ran back to camp with her still body in his arms, calling for Meriem to help. But Salambouha had given up her last breath.

Fifteen years later Salah's grief still remained, gnawing at his skin like an unhealed wound. There were times when it prevented him from sleeping and he suddenly aged as his grief all but consumed him. But in dying, Salambouha had left him with the finest gift she could ever bestow—a son, Mahmoud. He saw in this child the qualities and shortcomings of his beloved. Meriem was a competent guardian and had brought up the boy as her own, lavishing on him an abundance of affection. Mahmoud was a fearless child. At six he amused himself by catching horned vipers by the tail, until one day he was bitten on the ankle. Salah did everything he knew to save the child from the deadly poison that had flowed into his blood from the snake's fangs. He had first sucked the wound to draw out the venom and then he had placed a red-hot iron on the bite mark. Lastly, he had thrust the affected part of the child's leg into the open stomach of a freshly slaughtered dog while it still breathed. This barbarous remedy, used as a last resort, sometimes worked. And so it had for little Mahmoud, who emerged from his torpor forty-eight hours later.

To his credit, Mahmoud had not been a frail child. He was gifted with extraordinary strength and agility. He had no equal when it came to hanging on the tail of a running camel and allowing himself to be dragged along, feet in the dust, for fifty yards or so. When the animal lessened its pace from exhaustion he would unbalance and topple it by grabbing one of its hind legs. It was a dangerous exercise but a necessary step in mastering young camels to become part of the tribe's branded herd. Mahmoud equally excelled in vaulting. He could approach a trotting camel, grab its tail, and then jump onto the protruding part of its rear legs. He would then scramble from the croup onto the hump while the dromedary continued its course.

Whenever Salah saw these acrobatics he was apprehensive, but he swelled with pride at his son's display of courage and skill. Often Mahmoud would return to camp with cuts and bruises, only to be tended by Salah and Meriem, who would gently scold him. They begged that he leave this kind of activity to the camel drivers, but their entreaties only fell on deaf ears. Living with the camel herders, he learned how to interpret camel tracks in the sand, and how to determine the direction, load, and even the color or age of the animal. As a result, he became expert in recovering stray animals. After tirelessly traveling for many miles and posing inquiries at every camp, he would succeed in his quest for the lost camels. But Mahmoud had more than one string to his bow. He was an excellent shot, could write poetry, and on occasion would recite the verse of Saddoum, the great Reguibat bard.

This long reverie had kept Salah awake all night. Meriem, by his side, slept deeply. With his eyes open, Salah silently prayed. "O Allah, let Mahmoud return safely. I am ready to give my life for him." He dozed off finally, but was soon awakened by the voice of Abdallahi calling the faithful to the first prayers of the day. A pale light was creeping up in the east. As the Prophet said: "May Allah greet him and accord him blessings." It was the moment when it was possible "to distinguish a white thread from a black thread."

Salah rose and began to issue orders for breaking camp.

CHAPTER VIII

Hamoudi ould Himdoun came out of the tent with a look of exasperation. He ordered a *calabash* of water, which he then emptied over his head, snorting like a camel. He wiped his face and beard with his *chéche* and then returned to the circle of men who were dumbfounded by what they had just witnessed. The Reguibat generally avoid water, which they believe cause skin infections. They even go so far as to use sand for their ritual ablutions before prayer. So, by this dramatic act, Hamoudi succeeded in taming the tempestuous undercurrent of the meeting. He sat down and stared in turn at his fellow tribesmen with small, piercing eyes set in a long, bony face. Then he shouted:

"Enough! I don't want to hear any more of your criticism

and whining. It is not as though I were incapable. There is certainly no profit in being the leader of the Sellam and you must not insult me in this fashion. Do not forget that I am your chosen chief and that I have likewise won the approval of the administration. So I need say but one word to have you imprisoned. I demand respect, you hear me, respect!"

After a brief silence, he continued, still in the same tone:

"This, then, is the situation. You do stupid things and behave like idiots, while I'm the one who has to straighten matters out when something goes wrong."

Turning towards the victim's brothers, who sat with bowed heads in a corner of the tent, he said, "You are the five who arrived at the well? Mahmoud had one gun but you had two. How far away were you when he killed your brother?"

"About a hundred yards."

"And the four of you at a hundred yards' distance with two guns couldn't manage to intercept him?"

"We weren't expecting anything."

"When you heard the shot, why didn't you fire immediately in his direction? You knew that he was the one who had fired because your brother wasn't carrying a weapon. How did Mahmoud succeed in getting away? I know he's fast—he has a reputation for it—but all the same, you did have more firepower."

"Although we fired we couldn't hit him."

"You're miserable shots! How can you miss both a camel and a rider at one hundred yards? At my age I can still break an empty bottle at twice the distance! And afterwards, what did you do? Why didn't you try to catch him or were your camels too far off?"

"We thought we should bury our brother with dignity before alerting you."

"Yes, when I was 250 miles away at Tindouf! Are you still children? Wouldn't it have been more intelligent to alert the neighboring Sellam camp to get a few men together with arms and head towards Ain Ben Tili? Once there you could have presented your petition for satisfaction by firing shots into the air, to the general alarm of the district office. However, you chose to do nothing, and Mahmoud is proven to be smarter than you by turning himself in to the authorities. In doing so, he found refuge and thereby indirectly protected his father."

More calmly, Hamoudi added in an undertone:

"And he has also done the administration a big favor."

"How so?" asked Ghit.

Hamoudi looked discouraged at the lack of understanding on the face of his own lieutenant.

"I'll explain later," he said. "But I'll tell you this much: Larcher has acted in a remarkable manner. He's shown his cleverness by taking advantage of an awkward situation, forcing our negotiations."

Turning to the assembly again, he said:

"Now you turn to me to ask for your rights. As if by some miracle I could bring the victim back and bring you the head and heart of the murderer on a platter. What can I do?"

"What we must do," exclaimed Ghit ould Bouaha, "is apply the principle of 'an eye for an eye, a tooth for a tooth.' If Mahmoud is not executed we must select one of his brothers or another member of Salah's family."

"Really? Is it possible to say such things at your age?" Hamoudi interrupted angrily. "Think a moment. If you follow this principle, you'll be provoking a vendetta. Because, when you've killed a member of Salah's family, we will have to answer in blood. And this makes for a civil strife between the Sellam and the Sidi Allal. Battles at watering places. Constant insecurity. Fear in our caravans. Furthermore, the authorities would intervene to restore order. I can just picture squads of *meharistes* swarming into our camps. And what will we use for arms if there is not enough money? We must rule out retaliations in these circumstances because it is not in our best interests. Thanks to our cooperation with the French administration we are now free of the Sidi Allal. This would all have been in vain if the end result is only our massacre by these former masters."

The listeners were impressed by the logic of Hamoudi's reasoning. Taking advantage of this hard-won silence he continued:

"There is another way to provide for our rights and to obtain reparation. The alternative lies in asking for the price of blood. I should like the advice of one who is well informed about the law, Zein ould Omar."

All eyes turned towards a man about thirty-five years old sitting at one of the sides of the tent. He had not yet spoken. Zein was noted for the knowledge of customary and Koranic law that he had acquired among the Marabout Ma-El-Ainine in the Rio de Oro when he was young. He was a handsome man, with a statuesque head, an athletic, muscular body and a pair of very light blue eyes—a rare trait among the Reguibat. Zein had a gift for getting along equally well with both men and women. He had attained a noteworthy reputation and was greatly admired for his exploits with women, his eloquence, and his generosity despite the paucity of his herd.

Deliberately, Zein began to speak in a moderate tone.

"I, a humble camel driver, have nothing to add to the good sense and great clarity of insight offered by our beloved chief. Let us thank him for his bestowed wisdom in showing us the right path."

Hamoudi was flattered by this praise but wary as to what might ensue. However, he encouraged Zein to openly admit his feelings without being shy.

"Speak, Zein, without my having to beg you. Tell us what you know on the law of retaliation and the price of blood."

"As far as the law of retaliation is concerned," Zein began, "I understand, O Chief, that you cast the issue in a political light. Nonetheless I shall not be the one to pick holes in your argument. Quite the contrary. But I should like to make a few remarks as pertain to the legal issues."

"We're listening."

"The question is whether Mahmoud killed without a valid reason. Assuming he did, the law of retaliation applies with 'a soul for a soul.' His only way to escape is flight because the price of blood cannot be accepted. Did he commit deliberate homicide? The answer to this question has to be given by the assembly of notables, Ait Arbain—that is, forty persons of prominence chosen for their wisdom from among all the tribes of the confederation."

Hamoudi thought to himself: I don't want to become entangled with these legal minds. They always complicate everything. Then aloud he said:

"Speaking objectively, and strictly among ourselves, I feel that he killed for a valid reason. However, this shall not be made known to the Sidi Allal, since I intend to claim the contrary. But come to think of it, have you ever seen one man deliver insults to another who has a military advantage? Do you not agree with the logic of the outcome?"

He looked indifferently at the victim's brothers, who had covered their mouths with their *chèches* to indicate their refusal to reply.

Zein continued, "Then there is murder by provocation. The murderer must give everything he possesses to the family of the victim. The price of blood is 300 she-camels. If a Reguibat kills a stranger, his tribe—and even the entire confederation if need be—must help pay the debt. The third assumption applies to an unintentional homicide."

"Why not?" remarked Hamoudi. "Isn't anger unintentional? It is said that anger is blind."

"In this case, the tribe of the guilty man helps him to pay the blood price—100 she-camels, of whom one-third must be four years old, an equal measure three years old, and the remainder two years old. This does not exclude the *targuiba*, the gift of reparation to the victim's family, before any negotiation takes place. It consists of a sacrifice of between one and three adult camels."

There was a flood of questions from the men who had listened in admiration to Zein's answers for he gave the impression of knowing Moslem law down to the smallest details.

"A stab wound, torn clothes, scratched skin?"

"Payment of a *targuiba* of one to three camels," replied Zein, immediately.

"An eye?"

"The guilty one must give fifty she-camels to the injured man."

"An incisor tooth?"

"Five camels, four years old."

"A molar?"

"Eight camels, four years old."

"Robbery?"

"The thief pays four times the value of what he's stolen— twice as much to the owner and twice as much to the assembly of notables."

"In other words," Hamoudi broke in to end this game of question and answer, "we can choose one of three options in the case at hand. Number one, the murderer killed without a valid reason and is subject to the law of retaliation. Secondly, he could have provoked his victim before killing him, for which the blood price is 300 she-camels. Or, lastly, he killed unintentionally, for which he must pay 100 she-camels. Therefore, it is a question of interpretation with the assembly of notables acting in judgment. It is clear that this body has to decide."

Finally, to close the discussion he added, "Let's not forget that we have been victimized and that compensation is now our due."

Hamoudi's expectations were soon fulfilled. Towards the end of the afternoon, two visitors appeared at the campsite, Ali ould Abdi of the Lahcen ou Ahmed and Lemjed ould Bara of the Foqra. Hamoudi welcomed his guests with customary politeness but without much enthusiasm. As a representative of the victim's family, he was determined to maintain an aloofness. He did not care much for Ali ould Abdi, whose vanity was intolerable. On the other hand he had a favorable impression of Bara, a man with an impressive physique, his body covered with wounds from combat. He proudly sported his scars, which could be traced back to the earliest part of the century.

In an impassioned voice Ali ould Abdi began to explain the purpose of his mission before the men who had gathered in their chief's tent.

"The Reguibat are in mourning; they have lost one of their sons. It is you, the Sellam, who are the victims of an accident that Allah, whose designs are unfathomable, has brought about between brothers. Lemjed and I, as designated tribal chiefs, thought we could be influential in resolving the hostilities."

Hamoudi was silent as he pondered what lay behind these false sentiments. He speculated that Larcher had manipulated the two notables, making maximal use of their thirst for power. (Larcher had indeed sought out these men, who represented the two major factions in their society.) Lahcen ou Ahmed was from an independent tribe maintaining close ties with the Sidi Allal; the other leader was a member of an influential Foqra subgroup of the same rank as the Sellam.

Ali ould Abdi continued:

"We went to see the family of the murderer. Salah, who greets you and all men of good will, is saddened and sorely distressed. He asked us to convey to all the Legouacem his sorrow and condolences to the victim's family and to the Sellam."

Hamoudi began to be irritated by this tiresome, meaningless preamble as he waited impatiently for what was to follow.

Ali ould Abdi resumed after a brief silence:

"Salah ould Ahmed told us, 'Forget that I am the leader of the Sidi Allal and the spiritual head of the Legouacem Confederation. I am a Reguibi first. As the father of a murderer I intend to responsibly submit to the verdict delivered by the assembly of notables in accordance with our laws. I am in your hands and in Allah's. May it be as He wishes.' "

Hamoudi, interested now, asked:

"What does he mean by that? Would he abide by any decisions rendered by the council?"

"Yes. These are his intentions."

"Would he be willing to accept whatever verdict is reached— whether it be the law of retaliation or the price of blood?"

"Without a doubt. He made this point very clear," said Ali ould Abdi. "I repeated what he said word for word."

Ali ould Abdi's remarks were welcomed by the others and their murmurs of approval illustrated the power of his words. But Hamoudi was only partially satisfied. He was suspicious of Salah's apparent good intentions. By making a show of submitting to the law Salah was able to conceal his true motives. No doubt he would also attempt to bribe the assembly of notables to favor him. Also the ploy forced Hamoudi to accept the arbitration's eventual findings.

It was his turn to speak.

"The Sellam are in mourning. You are right in pointing this out. In their suffering they cannot think clearly. The suggestions offered by both you and Lemjed are commendable, and all the Sellam are grateful for them. We will submit to the decision handed down by the assembly of notables, but only with the provision that no member of the Sidi Allal be allowed to sit on the council."

"That goes without saying," Ali ould Abdi replied. "It will be the same for the victim's family. They will not have the right to participate since they might lack objectivity."

"But," Hamoudi urged, "it is important to know who will be attending the assembly you're organizing. As leader of the Sellam, I will be there with the council of my tribe. Will Salah ould Ahmed be there too?"

Ali hesitated before replying.

"Salah mentioned nothing about his attendance. Everything no doubt depends on his state of health."

"Don't make me laugh," retorted Hamoudi. "I am ready to bet that he will not attend but will be represented instead by someone of his tribe, outside of his family. As for the problems with his health, they haven't prevented him from moving to Moulay Mehdi's encampment in four days with women, children, baggage, and herds—it's a record time for that."

Lemjed ould Bara, who had not yet spoken, now broke in:

"That's not the main issue. The important thing is not only that the Sidi Allal agree in advance to submit to the council's verdict. They have pledged to do so before witnesses, and we are here to convey this information to you. So, with your cooperation, let us plan the itinerary of the meeting. We thought of convening the council at Bersigou with the families of the murdered man and the victim. It is only a few days' march from here and almost equidistant from the camps of the Sidi Allal and the Sellam. This way, each party will cover half the distance. Three weeks, we feel, is sufficient time to convene the assembly. What do you think?"

"The program suits me," Hamoudi acknowledged. "The Sellam will provide shelter and food in accordance with your requests. We will immediately start our preparations to arrive at Bersigou on the appointed day—you can count on us— Allah willing."

With an embarrassed smile, Lemjed added:

"I think it would be both useful and courteous to invite the authorities to attend the assembly as observers."

Hamoudi laughed heartily. As he had foreseen, the emissaries had received instructions from Larcher on this point. He would show that he was not so easily taken in.

"But of course. I see no objection in doing so. The Sellam have always displayed loyalty to France, is that not so?"

"Yes, perfectly true," admitted Lemjed. "We are now going

to submit to you the list of forty notables who should make up the council, a list already accepted by the Sidi Allal. You are free to reject any or all of the names in accordance with our customs."

Hamoudi found the list well balanced and had no special comment to make about it. His mind dwelled on how well things had thus far proceeded. But he still wondered what tactics old Salah would use to defend himself. His words indicated a readiness for an encounter with the Sellam. Hamoudi could not believe that his rival would agree to the price of blood without attempting to sway popular opinion. Obviously, the Sellam had to be vigilant and tough in the negotiations.

The sun had just set and it was the time for prayer. Hamoudi asked Lemjed to officiate. There followed a profusion of courtesies as Lemjed pretended to decline.

"The camp is honored by the presence of such a distinguished guest as yourself," Hamoudi complimented. "For myself and my men it would be a privilege for you to lead us in prayer this evening."

"I am but a common nomad," protested Lemjed. "But, as the proverb says, 'The visitor is in the hands of his host.' I will gladly serve as *imam* if you so desire."

CHAPTER IX

De La Renaudie was greatly surprised on arriving at the Bersigou camp with his two vehicles and a dozen native soldiers. He wondered how a people known for their untidiness and superficiality could manage to create such architectural harmony with impermanent dwellings. Twenty or more tents were situated at precise intervals comprising a semi-circle in a sandy hollow dominated by low, rounded hills. At the center of the encampment was a tent of imposing size which belonged to Lemjed ould Bara. Large enough to hold 100 persons, this dwelling served as the meeting place for the assembly of notables. De La Renaudie regretted having arrived too late to see the. tent being erected; it must have taken three camels to

transport it and at least six young women under the direction
of a matron to set it up. The Reguibat readily acknowledged
the important role of women in their society. "What would we
be without women?" they were in the habit of saying. "Women
are the guardians of our traditions and are responsible for
putting up our tents. In their absence we would sleep in the
open!" The French lieutenant, who was a good judge of things,
cast an approving eye at the quality of the woven tents, all
made of black goat hair which was tougher and more resistant
to rain than camel hair.

To be sure, all the tribes of the confederation had sent their
finest tents as well as their wisest men for the *Ait Arbain* or
Council of Forty. Larcher had chosen his chief of staff to
attend this assembly, which would affect intertribal relations
for many months. As commanding officer, Larcher wanted to
pursue an equitable policy. He was anxious to show the nomads that he would not intervene in their internal affairs.

He had decided to avoid the assembly to minimize any
official significance it might have. However, by sending his
senior aide, he made it clear that he was in sympathy with any
decisions of the Reguibat not detrimental to the administration.

When he arrived, de La Renaudie presented himself to the
dignitaries of the council. He congratulated Ali and Lemjed
for their efficient organization of the assembly. Hamoudi had
come in force with the Sellam tribesmen, and did not know
what the Sidi Allal's real intentions were. He grew increasingly
nervous waiting for their arrival. Would Salah come himself or
would someone be sent as his representative? The chosen
person would be either a member of the family or a prominent
outsider.

On the following day, after the noonday prayers, a mes-
senger presented himself to the men who were engaged in
desultory conversations within the tents. He announced the
imminent arrival of the Sidi Allal. The leading figures lined up
in a row, with the Sellam in the middle. Because all the nomads

were armed, de La Renaudie positioned his natives at strategic points. Hamoudi saw a dozen or so men at the entrance to the encampment who were now advancing with three adult camels. When they were about ten yards from the company, the Sidi Allal spontaneously formed a single line. One of them stepped forward and proceeded a few paces until he was opposite Hamoudi. There was an impressive silence, which he then shattered in a loud voice:

"O men! My name is Ahmed, eldest son of Salah ould Ahmed. In the absence of my brother, Mahmoud, who is at this moment under confinement, I come before you in the name of my father and put myself in your hands."

With these words Ahmed undid his cartridge belt, threw it to the ground, and laid his weapon on top of it. He continued:

"Here is my gun. Henceforth, it shall belong to the family of the victim. It is no longer mine. Here also are three adult camels that I offer as a *targuiba* by way of reparation. If you wish to kill me as the law allows, I am ready to atone for the errors of my brother. Kill me."

In a theatrical gesture, Ahmed ripped open the top of his robe with both hands to bare his chest. The silence that followed was broken by the sound of a rifle bolt being drawn back. At a swift sign from de La Renaudie, the native soldiers leaped on the victim's brother, who had slipped a bullet into his rifle. In a matter of seconds the man was disarmed. Ahmed had not flinched at the sound, but beads of perspiration stood out on his forehead. A murmur of admiration ran through the nobles at such a show of bravery. Hamoudi, disturbed, advanced towards Ahmed. The younger man then put his right hand on Hamoudi's head as a sign of submission and said:

"You are the offended; I am the offender, servant of Allah."

Hamoudi put his arm round the other's shoulders, according to custom took his hand, and spoke:

"Welcome. You are my son and you are under my protection."

The two men disappeared into the central tent, followed by

the assemblage. The tension and emotion of these last few moments were broken as all the participants embraced, slapped one another on the back, and conversed loudly. Afterwards Hamoudi, attended by Ahmed and Lemjed, gave orders. Ahmed, with an inborn sense of duty, had earned his title to nobility. He had shown dignity and courage in adhering to convention. Hamoudi, who had not expected Salah to send his eldest son as envoy, was extremely pleased. He had become the recipient of public reparation from Salah, reinforcing his credibility within the tribe. Yet something was bothering him. He still did not understand Salah's attitude. The old chief, despite being absent, still seemed to be the one in control; he had reaped the benefits of a skillfully executed scenario staged by his son. Hamoudi decided to probe Ahmed as to his intentions.

"It is rather late this evening to begin the council meeting. Let us drink tea and feast together as a pledge of friendship."

"It has been agreed," replied Ahmed, "that I shall not be taking part in the council's deliberations. My father, who respects customary law, has forbidden me to do so. Our interests will be represented by Hassan ould Bouali of the Belgacem ou Brahim, who has received very precise instructions for the negotiations. I have not even been briefed on these matters."

The cleverness of the move was not lost on Hamoudi. Salah, under the pretext of obeying their customs, had as a safeguard divided his defensive strategy among several individuals. Ahmed had been designated as the sacrificial victim without his being party to any crucial knowledge. Although intelligent and clever, he was lacking in negotiating ability. This was not the case with Hassan, whose presence was felt in a corner of the tent, where he sat with an elegant and well-groomed but quite expressionless appearance.

The next day, after the first prayer had been intoned, the council members took their places in Lemjed's tent with the obligatory solemnity. Lemjed, as the appointed assembly president, said a few words of welcome. He then gave the floor to Hamoudi, who represented the injured party.

"I shall be brief," Hamoudi began. "As you all know, the murderer's family openly admits to the deed. Of this there is no doubt. The Sellam are cognizant of the Sidi Allal's willingness to accept the judgment delivered by this august assembly. It is therefore your task to decide upon the penalty."

Hassan ould Bouali was the next speaker. In a dispassionate voice he began:

"I fully concur with Chief Hamoudi. This meeting should be characterized by mutual understanding and meditation. In a gesture of good will, we have offered a sizable *targuiba* reparation of three adult camels. Although not demanded of us, we are also generously offering a gun. However, in the name of Salah, of whom I am the representative, we shall make no further concessions. Of course, we have no objection to polemics, and we will take under consideration their result without being duty bound to heed it."

These words produced astonishment in the assembly and indignation among the Sellam. Hamoudi, somewhat perturbed, said:

"May we know what makes the Sidi Allal opposed to the proceedings that will follow?"

"The answer is simple," Hassan replied. "Our discussions are abstract. Mohammed ould Souilem is dead and so is Mahmoud, his murderer."

"How do you mean?" asked Hamoudi, getting more and more irritated.

"Mahmoud has been taken by the French authorities, a situation over which we have no control. His disappearance from the Reguibat territory has provided us with an enigma as to his whereabouts. His father, Salah, considers him dead; justice has been done. Can anyone here deny what I have related?"

Hamoudi was holding his head between his hands. How

could he neglect to anticipate this strategy? Salah had deceived him once again by agreeing to the wishes of the council, and in offering the generous *targuiba* which included a gun. Furthermore, he had cunningly refused to accept any judgment by the assembly on the pretext that his son had disappeared! The logic was indisputable. Doubtless, most of the forty council members would be upset over this turn of events. With grim determination, Hamoudi resolved to confront his opposition. He raised his hand for permission to speak, and the buzz of voices ceased.

"In other words, the great spiritual and temporal leader of all the Reguibat, the respected guardian of our values, refuses to pay the price of blood!"

Hassan, without elevating his voice, quickly rejoined:

"I ask the victim's family—whose grief is understandable— not to judge rather hastily or to censure the motives of Salah. I also feel that our discussion should approximate some semblance of tranquility, and if such conduct cannot be maintained I would prefer to withdraw.

"However, I would like to remind you that Salah has indicated from the beginning that he would willingly pay the price of blood. He has told the intermediaries so, an intention that I am reiterating today. But why should you want a man to pay the price of blood twice over, once to the French administration and again to the victim's family?"

The noise and commotion reached such a pitch that Lemjed was obliged to call for silence. Then he began to speak:

"I respect Hassan ould Bouali's ideas, but we must not be unintentionally swayed by such reasoning. Although reference has been made to Mahmoud's disappearance, he is at this very moment in a French prison. And he is very much alive, while Mohammed is dead."

There was an approving silence. Hamoudi raised his head and Lemjed continued:

"The Council of Forty has not been summoned without just

provocation. It first has to decide on the particulars of the murder and on what penalty is to be exacted. This is not the place for blood feuds. The Sidi Allal can view the judgment according to their conscience and that decision is solely theirs.

"I shall ask the Sellam and the Sidi Allal to return to their respective tents while deliberations are in progress. The final judgment will be conveyed by two of the council members, who will prompt each tribe to abide by our decision. Let us resume the discussions after the afternoon's prayers.

"Before the deliberations, I should like to question the French representatives about the method of Mahmoud's trial and whether there is any eventuality of his return."

De La Renaudie discretely replied:

"I thank Lemjed for the honor of addressing this august body. The administration does not want to interfere with your laws or religion. Out of deference to your traditions I am only in attendance as an impartial observer.

"It is not my place to engage in partisan politics. As far as Mahmoud is concerned, I should like to repeat that he is in the hands of the law and his fate will be decided accordingly. I have no prescient knowledge regarding the verdict or the date of Mahmoud's return. There is nothing more that I can say at this juncture."

De La Renaudie could see that his response was acceptable to the Sidi Allal. But it was important not to discredit French law or to dwell on the extenuating circumstances surrounding the case. Larcher had given him very firm instructions pertaining to these matters. The session ended, with the Sidi Allal and the Sellam returning to their respective tents at either end of the camp.

Hamoudi was furious, but Hassan was pleased. The council seemed to have been impressed with Hassan's specious reasoning. He had made an impact on his listeners without yet offering concessions that would undermine Salah's prestige. He decided to bide his time. Later, when the two emissaries came from the council to inform him that the price of blood had been fixed at 100 she-camels, he remained cool. He refused to offer any comment on the proposed settlement.

When the assembly met again in the late afternoon, around five, Hassan sensed that now was the time to end his intransigence. And so he began:

"I cannot repeat enough that Salah does not want to pay a double blood-price. If Mahmoud were among us it would be different and we would have submitted immediately to the council's decision. However, out of respect for the council we have decided as a gesture of good will to make an offering of twenty-five she-camels to the victim's family."

These words were welcomed enthusiastically by the council members who had been on the verge of despair over reaching any acceptable compromise. Hamoudi, once again, was caught off balance. It would seem that Salah was to exhibit his superiority by paying only one-fourth of the designated sum. Such an offer was humiliating and ought to be rejected out of hand. Hamoudi was still smoldering at being put on the spot by the Sidi Allal's carefully planned maneuver. The arrogance with which Hassan had made the offer! The amused look on his face! The mocking smile that showed on his lips! But Hamoudi felt that inflexibility would lose him the support of his own people. The victim's family, lured by the prospect of immediate gain, urged him to accept. He also perceived that after endless negotiations the *Ait Arbain* was positively euphoric at reaching a decision.

He asked the president for the floor.

"I would like to question whether these twenty-five she-camels are to be considered part of the blood-price or as a peace offering."

The question was a clever one, and Hassan had some difficulty answering:

"It is a gesture of good will on the part of the Sidi Allal, who do not make such an offering as a fulfillment of the blood-price. But in the event that they were to honor the latter at a future date, then this initial payment would be taken into account."

Hamoudi followed his argument closely, reading the implicit statements that it concealed.

"If I have understood you correctly, the victim's family, whose interest I am here to protect, may consider part of the blood-price paid towards the prospective total?"

Hassan was suspicious but he conceded the point. "Certainly, the family may interpret matters in this fashion."

Hamoudi resumed. "Then, under the circumstances, if Mahmoud came back, the Sellam could demand the price of blood to be paid in full, counting the twenty-five she-camels it will already have received, of course."

Hassan saw the trap and he countered his opponent's thrust: "If Mahmoud returned, I should propose convening another assembly to determine a new blood-price based on whatever penalties had already been paid by the Sidi Allal to the French."

Hamoudi was pleased at this prospect for he had achieved his secret aim of keeping the case open, thereby saving face. Now he would attempt to beat Hassan on his own ground.

"All in all, the results are not satisfying. I wish to state for the record that the Sellam have not had their due." He spoke the words emphatically, pounding the rug with his hand. The assembly was silent.

He paused for a moment, and then continued:

"Nevertheless, I appreciate the integrity of the council members in their efforts to aid my people. I therefore accept Hassan's offer, which I feel should be payable immediately. I shall consider it to be an initial payment—one-fourth the total price of blood set by the council. To facilitate the task of collection, I propose that the assembly include the *targuiba* offered by the murderer's family."

There was a moment of stupefaction when the listeners

heard these words. But Hamoudi, unperturbed, continued:

"I therefore suggest that four camels be deducted from the total, the fourth as compensation for the price of the gun. This will leave twenty-one she-camels as the final payment, which is in keeping with our law. According to our statutes there must be three she-camel lots: seven four-year-olds, seven three-year-olds, and seven two-year-olds."

Hamoudi realized that he would be reproved by his own people, but he wanted to make a gesture of generosity equal to such earlier deeds of their former masters, the Sidi Allal.

CHAPTER X

Senhouri uttered a low groan as each lash of the whip fell on his bare, emaciated chest. The well-muscled Reguibi was savagely taking pleasure in flailing the captive Jakani, who crouched on the ground. "You dog, you son of a dog, you filthy black bastard, speak," he shouted, slicing the air with the whip. As it landed, the pitiful body writhed with pain. Mantallah, Senhouri's twelve-year-old son, was also bound and could only watch the scene helplessly. He alternately sobbed and shouted, but his father's tormentor took not the slightest notice of him. One final deadly blow brought forth a shriek from Senhouri, who collapsed unconscious. He lay motionless on the ground, his chest bleeding profusely. Mantallah gave a long cry like a hyena at night in an abandoned camp. The Reguibi, surprised, rewarded him with a single lash that left a dark red weal on the boy's body.

Mantallah woke with a start from his sleep. His expression was haggard; his chest heaved; his shirt clung to his sweat-drenched body. Even though he was now thirty-two years old, he still had nightmares in which he relived the anguish of this incident twenty years before.

In common with most of the Tajakant of his generation, Senhouri had made his living as a caravaneer. The trade was lucrative. Tindouf, founded in 1852 by Sheikh M'Rabet ould Belamech, was still a flourishing oasis at the beginning of the century. The caravans at this time, sometimes numbering 500 men, carried salt, incense, ostrich feathers, henna, leather, gold, ivory, silver, and Bambaras slaves to Morocco. On returning to the southern Sahara they were laden with cotton fabrics, coral, copper, and tea. In 1914, however, Tindouf was overcome by the Reguibat, who sought out its great wealth. Senhouri managed to flee south with his family and set up a home in Timbuktu as well as he could. He continued to lead small caravans to Morocco, always managing to stay ahead of Reguibat raiders. Then, one ominous day in January 1930, four years before the French arrival, Senhouri succumbed to the dreaded *rezzou*. He had yielded to his young son Mantallah's pleadings to accompany him on his journey. He wanted to show the boy his skills and teach him something of his craft.

After a few days' uneventful march the caravan, consisting of ten camels and their drivers, arrived at a watering place in the Hank known as Chega. They stopped there before crossing the vast plain the nomads likened to a gigantic sheet of smooth, blank paper. The plain led to Erg Iguidi, and from there to Morocco, veering away from Tindouf, which lay further to the east. At the well Senhouri became anxious. Tracks around the waterhole bore evidence that a group of some fifty camel riders, traveling light, had recently stopped to water their

The Camel Rider

animals. Who could they be if not Reguibat nomads that were in quest of caravans to be easily plundered? Senhouri decided to conceal all the valuable merchandise they were carrying— gold, silver bars, leather, incense, and ostrich feathers. With the help of his son and a trusted companion he securely deposited them in crevices among the rocks. In the event of attack, the Reguibat would seize only the less valuable goods. He planned to retrieve the cache on his next journey.

But in his precautionary measures Senhouri committed what was to become a fatal error. The next day, when the caravan had come down from the cliffs and was on the edge of the great plain, the leading camel driver shouted: "The Reguibat!" Like a flight of vultures with outstretched wings, their robes billowing in the wind, some fifty men on fast camels swooped on all sides. Shouting and firing their guns, they encircled the tiny convoy. Senhouri, seeing the numerical superiority of his assailants, tried to prevent four of his companions from opening fire. But they could not be restrained, and they brought down first one nomad and then another. Greatly angered, some of the attackers jumped from their camels and stabbed the four Tajakant before they had time to reload. The other members of the caravan were taken as captives. When the conquering leader inspected the caravan he immediately realized that a sizeable amount of valuable merchandise was absent. In his frustration he began beating Senhouri to make him reveal the places of concealment. But Senhouri remained silent until he fainted from the repeated blows. By nightfall, he had regained consciousness and called in a feeble voice to his son, who was nearby.

"I am finished. I sense that I am going to die soon. You must try to escape. Take a camel with enough water and some of the provisions concealed within the rocks. Go back to your mother, brothers, and sisters in Timbuktu."

While the guards slept, the boy dragged himself close to Senhouri and was freed of his bonds by his father's strong teeth. Mantallah, now unencumbered, wanted to save his father, who was forcefully prodding him to flee. The boy kissed his father, crept through the sleeping camp, and made good his escape. After an exhausting journey on a camel stolen from the Reguibat he succeeded in reaching Timbuktu.

Mantallah had sworn to avenge his father. Although a rather poor rifle marksman, he excelled in knife throwing. For years, day in and day out, he rehearsed exactly what he would do when he confronted his father's murderer. Eight years later, almost at the very same spot, Allah had fulfilled his wishes. Stopping at the Chega well for water one day, he had seen the very man he was looking for. Mantallah came within ten yards or so of his foe and addressed him:

"I am Mantallah ould Senhouri, son of the leader of the caravan whom you murdered at the foot of this cliff. I ask Allah for atonement in blood."

The Reguibi made a grab for the rifle that was slung over his shoulder, but Mantallah moved faster and had already hurled his dagger with lightning speed. The blade struck the man full in the chest and brought him to the ground, choking and gasping in agony. Without hurrying, Mantallah went up to his victim, insulted him, then calmly turned his head in the direction of Mecca and slit his throat. As he did so, he spoke the ritual words as if he had been slaughtering an animal. With no one else nearby, Mantallah concealed the body and the gun, freeing the Reguibi's camel to join the herd.

This vendetta was small consolation for the death of his father, whose remains had been identified by an amulet found on a skeleton in the desert. He had given a proper burial to Senhouri and his fallen companions. With the arrival of the French, Mantallah returned to Tindouf with his family and resumed his trade as a caravaneer. His personality and enviable reputation had attracted most of the exiled Tajakant as immigrants to their formal capital. The oasis, deserted in 1934, had become a prosperous center and the home of 2,000 Tajakant. There was a concerted revival of the fine Saharan houses characterized by inner courtyards and colonnades. Mantallah had quickly realized the beneficial influence of the French in restoring the Tajakant's rights and territories. He had therefore displayed unsurpassed loyalty and devotion to the administration.

It was going to be a red-letter day for Mantallah. It was ironic that he, the village head, should receive the Reguibat leader, a direct descendant of those who had destroyed Tindouf forty years earlier. That evening he would give a great feast on his terrace for fifty guests, including the leading figures of the tribes and the French administration. For the occasion he had donned a pale-blue robe with embroidered pockets complemented by a dark-blue turban.

About ten o'clock twenty elite Tajakant gathered in front of their chief's house, the embarkation point for their meeting with Salah at the market. Mantallah, looking at his men's faces, could not repress the smile that was emerging.

"Come, there's no need for these expressions. I know what you are thinking and how you must feel deep down. But we're the ones who will come out ahead."

The oldest man in the group spoke out without hesitation.

"I believe that this whole business is most useful for your prestige and personal renown, but that doesn't help us."

Mantallah had to control himself or he would have exploded. Then he answered in a disarming voice:

"I have been chosen as your delegate to the French, but if one of you wishes to change places with me I will offer no resistance. I will do honor to the dictates of my people."

"We will follow you," came a chorus of voices.

"So don't complain about my activities. It is my responsibility as mayor to welcome traveling dignitaries. We have been at peace with the Reguibat for over twenty years and it is incumbent upon us to welcome them as visitors."

"Yes, that's clear," the others assented.

The Caid of Tindouf with his people.

"But let me just say one thing because I know what you must be thinking. Although we are now in agreement you feel I am unnecessarily zealous in welcoming our former enemies. But you cannot see the hidden reasoning that belies my seeming amicability. In the eyes of the Reguibat we are lowly black slaves, good only for exploitation. Salah has not been to Tindouf in six years, and I want to prove that the Tajakant have grown strong and are united. They have rebuilt their village and become prosperous; we are now the Reguibat's equal."

The eloquent words were greeted with shouts of approval from the other men. Old Jakani broke in:

"Forgive me, my chief, if I offended you. I now understand the reasons behind this ceremony, and you have earned our unanimous approval. We often criticized you for working so closely with the French administrators, but we can appreciate that such liaisons are necessary for the betterment of our welfare."

"Why do you dislike France when she has given us such security?"

"This may be true, but the French occupy our land and they are unbelievers. They do not belong to the Dar El Islam, to the Islamic world. We cannot therefore accept them."

"And the Reguibat?"

"One Frenchman is worth more than ten Reguibat. We hate the Reguibat from the depths of our hearts. But, as you said so fervently, we must put aside any ill-feeling and accept them as our brothers."

Mantallah, satisfied with this illuminating discourse, concluded:

"Therefore we all understand that France's presence means opportunity for the Tajakant; without France we would be helpless. We must utilize the situation to our best advantage, enhancing our position as France's spokesmen. While the Reguibat are facing the setting sun, ours is only yet on the horizon."

With these words Mantallah gave the signal for the group to advance toward the market, only a few hundred yards distant. He assigned the various functions: according to custom, his two sons would present the guests with milk and dates; ten men would fire into the air—three rounds per rifle; and a group of musicians with tambourines, drums, and flutes would play joyful melodies during the welcoming ceremony.

At eleven o'clock Salah ould Ahmed appeared with an impressive entourage. He had left his camel at the palm plantation and then continued on to the market by foot. The rifle salute was given, the music started, and Mantallah came forward. The two men embraced in accordance with custom while a reception committee welcomed the Reguibat contingent. Salah took a sip of milk, ate a date, and, visibly moved, waited for Mantallah to speak. The Tajakant leader resolutely uttered the words of welcome:

"Welcome to my family, Salah ould Ahmed, leader of the Confederation of the Reguibat Legouacem. May Allah's salvation and blessing be upon you. Greetings to your companions.

"Mantallah ould Senhouri welcomes you this day. All the Tajakant are descended from the great family of Coraich and Abou-Bakr-Es-Sediq, the first caliph of Islam, father-in-law of Mohammed, our Prophet. May Allah grant him salvation and His blessing."

Mantallah paused; the Reguibat waited impassively. Then he continued:

"This day will become history. Never could our fathers have imagined such a meeting, which has been made possible by a twenty-year peace between our two peoples. May Allah let it continue for centuries more. Know, honored Salah, that we shall do what we can to further this union and we bid you welcome to enjoy the fruits of our labors."

Mantallah came to the end of his speech. He was filled with pride at recalling the noble origins of his people. It was then Salah ould Ahmed's turn to speak.

"O Tajakant, thank you for your magnificent welcome,

which goes straight to our hearts. You know the nomads. They are like birds on a branch. They are happy to find a nest such as Tindouf with its boundless hospitality. O chief, I congratulate you on what has been accomplished in such a short space of time. The village has been transformed; it is well populated and prosperous. Trade is brisk and joy is in evidence everywhere. Let us give thanks to the Lord. Let us be grateful to Him for having put an end to the quarrels between us and to our fratricidal feuding. Tajakant, you are our brothers, our equals, and our friends. Never in my lifetime, I swear, will you have to suffer through any fault of ours. You know that I am a man of peace, and as proof I drank of your milk and ate of your dates. May Allah's grace be upon you and your families."

Mantallah now took Salah's hand and, preceded by stately music, led his guest into the village. On the terraces, the women ululated joyfully while armed men fired into the air. Salah, agreeably surprised by this welcome, allowed himself to be guided by Mantallah, who was perfectly at home in the maze of twisting, sand-swept streets lined with handsome earth-walled houses. At last they emerged onto a small square before a mosque; a single-story house stood before them. Mantallah spoke:

"This is your house, Salah; view it as you would your own home. I have had rugs laid in every room and two servants will be at your disposal. You will find all the provisions you could wish for."

They entered the house. A series of rooms gave onto a spacious court enclosed by a high wall. A new tent had been erected in the center. Salah thanked his host.

"I'm afraid that my visit, which I had planned to be short, may extend beyond the norms of politeness," he said by way of compliment. "You have even remembered to erect a tent in which I may sleep at night. It is somewhat ridiculous but I find myself unable to sleep in a house when a tent beckons. But what else would be correct for a nomad? I was born and will die as such."

The two men wished each other happiness and Mantallah repeated his invitation for dinner that evening. He then withdrew with his companions. Salah entered the tent, sat down cross-legged, and ordered tea. He summoned his son, Ahmed, and Hassan ould Bouali, his adviser.

"What do you think of this welcome?" he inquired of them.

"It is rather surprising on the part of the Tajakant since they hate us bitterly for the wrong we did them twenty years ago," replied Hassan. "This welcome shows above all that Mantallah has the makings of a leader. He is intelligent and clever in taking moral revenge on his former enemies this morning."

"That's exactly what I thought," said Salah. "Although I have very little esteem for a people that earn their living in caravan trading, I am reminded of their merit and tenacious sense of community. I am a man of peace and deeply regret that Moslems should have massacred and destroyed villages belonging to others of their faith. Of course, our fathers did not share the same philosophy, but the injustices committed against the Tajakant were shameful nonetheless. I have come here to make the acquaintance of the French commander even though it is degrading for one of my stature to initiate this contact. In fact, did anyone see an officer at the welcoming ceremony?"

"No doubt Larcher was deliberately responsible for their absence," remarked Hassan. "Larcher wants the nomads and the sedentary tribes to think that he does not wish to intervene in their internal affairs. He has left intact some remote semblance of autonomy. Obviously his policy has succeeded, with the new administrators purported to be popular among the people."

"Yes, I understand," commented Salah. "But how am I going to meet the commander? I am embarrassed to present myself assertively, even if it is only out of politeness. Or should I wait until he summons me—but what could be more humiliating? There is nothing covetous in what I say. Intruding upon Larcher would humble and detract from my bearing."

"You have nothing to fear on that score, Father," Ahmed replied. "According to all reports from Mantallah's entourage, Larcher and his officers are invited this evening to the same dinner as we are."

"That is a good idea," replied Salah. "We will find ourselves on neutral ground, with the least thought given to the matter of my introduction. If, however, Larcher attempts to dispense with formalities and begins upon the subject of my son, I will leave immediately."

"Sir, I think we can trust this officer."

"I hope so."

Changing the subject abruptly, Salah questioned Hassan:

"I didn't quite understand Mantallah's reference to the Coraich. Are the Tajakant really descended from this noble tribe and from the first caliph of Islam? It's amusing to consider the implications."

"That's what they say," replied Hassan, smiling, "but who would contradict them? They are trying to establish their nobility. However, I don't believe a word. I'm inclined to think they are descendants of Saharan Berber tribes belonging to the group of veiled Lemtouna Canhadja."

"That explanation seems more probable," Salah commented, laughing heartily. "People are funny. Why should they all want to go back to the Prophet? May Allah grant him salvation and His blessings. It is a blasphemy. In our own case Sid Ahmed Reguibi is the source of our ancestral name, which is more than sufficient for us."

CHAPTER XI

Larcher put on his *kepi* and rejoined the four officers waiting outside the bedroom.

"Let's go. Mantallah said eight o'clock and we should be on time. The mayor has been considerate enough to invite us at the same hour as Salah. No doubt this was no accident but an idea implanted by Vogel."

"Not at all," said Vogel with a smile.

"You can't fool me, but you did well. The first meeting is going to be on neutral ground with a formal grouping of witnesses. It's perfect, but what do you suggest for the primary topic of conversation? I think we should desist from demanding anything further of him since he has already submitted to coming here. Do you think he will ask to see me?"

"He may request an appearance, since this has been upper-most in his mind, and it is customary that he visit the residing dignitary," suggested de La Renaudie.

"Under the circumstances, I shall invite him, as well as his son and adviser, to lunch at my house."

"He will be delighted," Vogel added, "especially if the invitation is delivered in a loud voice before fifty or more people this evening. It would be even more becoming if he does not have to degradingly present himself at your office after being announced by one of your orderlies."

"Another thing," Larcher noted. "We must allow no reference to a burnoose or a red cape. Any allusion to these things would be disastrous."

"We will have to bring the matter up sooner or later," Vogel said.

"I will instruct you as to a more suitable vocabulary to use then," replied Larcher. "You might start thinking about some alternative Arabic words yourself. But above all, I don't want any of you to mention this matter tonight, or it may spoil everything. We must remember what implications may result from a premature disclosure."

The five officers set off for Mantallah's house while Larcher continued his dialogue.

"I don't want to keep anything from you—I always feel a little uneasy about going to Mantallah's. Not that the evening or the food won't be pleasant. Quite the contrary, the meal will be superbly cooked and his wife is quite a hostess. However, the man does pose a problem."

"What is it that disturbs you?" inquired de La Renaudie.

"Nothing that I can define, and that's what bothers me. It would be difficult to find anyone more cooperative or enthusiastic in helping us."

"In other words," de Vignandeau exclaimed, "you would have preferred someone who dealt more reluctantly with the French."

"To be sure he is the picture of amicability with his little goatee, Oriental eyes, and constantly fixed smile. His head bears resemblance to an inscrutable Chinese Mandarin. And he's a man of great physical and moral agility. He may be small and frail-looking, but inside he is a man of iron. He could be very useful to us, but he fully realizes that his loyalty could well cost him the support of his fellow tribesmen. They already hold us in such low esteem—an assessment we shouldn't have any illusions about. What will become of him if we leave?"

"I think," Vogel explained, "that we need not worry too much about him. In this outward display of loyalty to France, Mantallah is really pursuing his own interests. Although the Tajakant think little of him, they are nonetheless grateful. He has the mentality of someone who has risen in life and is determined to settle a score. In fact, he is attempting to elevate the status of his tribe at the expense of the Reguibat. If independence comes, the nomads will now have to fight sedentary tribes that are better organized and informed than they are. By accepting us, Mantallah has shown great foresight and wisdom."

"That's an overly generalized view of things," Larcher noted. "Anyway, we have not reached that point yet. And besides, our reception is far too generous to find fault."

Chatting about one thing and another, the small group of officers soon arrived at the entrance to the mayor's house, who was now awaiting them. After the customary greetings, Mantallah, who wore the cross of the Legion of Honor, led the way down a narrow corridor that gave on to the terrace. The first floor was surrounded by a gallery, where the officers paused momentarily to view the outstretched scene. In the square courtyard below them several fires had been lit in preparation for the evening's meal. Women glided between the fires, their veiled silhouettes furtively caressing the walls of the patio, which were faintly lit by oil lamps. Over sunken pits filled with glowing embers, three whole sheep turned gently on their spits. A steady ribbon of steam escaped from under the covers of earthenware pots. Enormous round containers, made of pewter, held mountains of *couscous*, hand-milled semolina that had been coated with butter. Casseroles and cauldrons of every size sat on separate braziers away from the main cooking area. In them simmered sauces and vegetables to complement the main dishes.

An assortment of highly appetizing, distinctive smells wafted upwards. Piquant spices mingled with the smoke of grilled meat and the subtle fragrance of aromatic herbs— thyme, coriander, basil, and mint.

With the arrival of the French officers, those guests that were already seated on the terrace rose in a respectful and heartfelt silence. The mayor, as befitted his station, began the introductions. He and the commander saluted each individual, one by one. Then the guests spread out among the low round tables and sat down on the rugs, crossing their legs in the usual fashion. Larcher found himself seated between Salah and Mantallah. After a highly seasoned tomato-based soup, the parade of *tajines* began. The name refers to both the contents and the containers of Moroccan dishes, consisting of meat with an assortment of various vegetables. In general, the ingredients were in accordance with established recipes, distinguished by certain modifications on the part of each cook. There was a murmur of admiration as servants swiftly removed the heavy, conical covers on the glazed earthenware. A mixture of winsome scents escaped from the amalgam of vegetables and meat that had simmered together slowly for several hours. A *tajine* of chicken with potatoes, onions, leeks, and tomatoes was followed by a similarly styled *tajine* of pigeon with an additional layer of dried raisins. To end the first course there was a *tajine* of baby-camel meat with prunes.

Next came the three roasted sheep carried in on their spits and placed on table cloths to protect the rugs. These *mechouis*, to use the Arabic word, had been prepared in the Algerian manner of open-air charcoal cooking, rather than in an oven, the common practice in Morocco. The master of the house rose and began to tear off strips of the crisp skin, which he distributed among his guests. Larcher, who had learned from past experience, made a dive for the sheep's eyes and with an adroit movement of his fingers scooped them out of their sockets, only to present the offerings to his neighbors, who swallowed them with gusto. He had, in effect, made a gesture of courtesy that was much appreciated, for the sheep's eyes were a delicacy always reserved for the guests of honor. At the same time he had avoided the obligatory role of consuming them himself, something he had not yet learned to do without a certain repugnance. Larcher then extracted with considerable dexterity the fleshy part above the jaw, of which he was particularly fond.

Always with their right hands, the diners began to take the chunks of lamb that Mantallah cut in large, juicy portions, using his dagger so as not to burn his fingers. The connoisseurs showed little interest in the drier parts, particularly the legs. They waited with a feigned air of detachment for the flanks of the carcass to be sufficiently exposed. This revealed the tenderloin around the spine, the kidneys cooked in their own grease, and finely textured meat between the shoulder blades and the ribs. Meanwhile, sweet and sour whey was served in large wooden calabashes, then passed from hand to hand to quench the guests' thirst.

After the carcasses of the sheep had been removed, enormous dishes piled high with golden *couscous* were brought in. Mantallah had chosen to serve the grain in the Algerian manner. It was accompanied by a generous heaping of sauce, spicy or mild, with vegetables that had been cooked separately—chick peas, sweet pimentos, carrots, turnips, onions, and pieces of mutton. The guests, using the first three fingers of their right hands as a scoop, quickly demolished the mounds. They kneaded the grain in their palms, shaping it into a little ball, and finally flicking it decisively into their mouths with the back part of the thumb. Next Mantallah ordered a platter of Moroccan-style *couscous* to be brought in. This time the dish was made with a finer grain and garnished with raisins, cinnamon, and powdered sugar laid across the semolina in wide colored swathes. The diners, already full, scarcely touched this last dish, which was sent back to the kitchen immediately.

The hot, fragrant mint tea that was served next was a welcome beverage after such a feast. Afterwards, a servant circulated with a pitcher of hot water, a towel, and an enormous copper bowl for the waste water. The guests, who had already run their grease-smeared fingers over the soles of their feet as a balm for their cracked and craggy skin, now washed their hands with hot water poured from the pitcher held aloft. Some of them took advantage of the pure, clear water to rinse their mouths and clean their teeth, rubbing their gums with index fingers and spitting out the water with loud gurgling noises.

Contrary to what he had feared, Larcher found Salah to be an agreeable companion. Somewhat reserved at the beginning, the leader of the Legouacem grew more relaxed when he realized that the commander was not going to touch upon sensitive problems or make reference to Salah's extended absence from Tindouf.

The conversation centered on the respective merits of nomadic and sedentary cooking. For the Bedouins, Salah explained, food is consumed primarily for subsistence rather than pleasure. The sedentary tribes, on the contrary, view cooking as part of their comfortable lifestyle. It is easy to understand why the caravans cannot carry heavy utensils or fragile and delicate ones such as earthenware dishes. So the Reguibat use pots and pans made of tin that soon become dented when the nomads are on the move. Even making a fire is a problem in the desert since wood is scarce and is limited mostly to dried grass roots and a few branches of dead trees. Lastly, the nomad woman, unlike her sedentary sister, can seek no refuge from the wind while performing her open-air cooking. For these reasons food among the nomads is reduced to the utmost simplicity. It may consist of fresh or cured camel and antelope meat, milk and milk products—whey, fresh and rancid butter. Another basic foodstuff is barley, which is ground into flour with a portable mill consisting of two flat stones that turn one on top of the other. Often the barley is grilled and the flour mixed with leftover dried meat. When traveling it is a simple matter to pour boiling water onto this mixture, turning it into a paste which is then moistened by a small lump of camel grease.

Having described his people's cuisine, Salah then explained that the nomads could not regularly eat the rich foods of the sedentary tribes. If they did, they would soon be smitten with *iguendi*, a malady whose symptoms included vertigo, excessive sweating, aching muscles, and signs of deafness. It was caused by salt, spices, and pepper in the food. De Vignandeau confirmed Salah's statements. *Iguendi* belonged to a category of disorders symptomatic of a vitamin deficiency. When the body is undernourished its stability is easily disturbed, resulting in cellular dehydration. This is particularly observable when large quantities of sodium chloride are ingested, as is the custom in the Western Sahara. The ubiquitous presence of this spice in water supplies seems to predispose one to *iguendi*. A viable remedy consists of a diet rich in protein and lipids. However, it seems difficult to effect a treatment among people grown used to this deficiency in the course of their lifetimes.

The conversation turned next to the weather, a topic that Salah was most objective about. The year had yet to see heavy rains, with the fall not issuing forth with one overcast day. The onset of winter had not answered people's hopes. The few showers had barely, as the expression went, "washed the bushes and the mouths of the locusts." Although the camels had been provided with water from residual pools and man-made ground wells, they had by now lost their big humps. However, there was general optimism about the spring rains. Cumulous cloud formations that evening were perhaps indicative of better weather. The winds from the north and west had dropped; they had been replaced by winds from the south and east, which were much more promising. Rain often accompanied the east wind. The Legouacem called it "the fertilizer from the sky." But there was no resisting the south wind; when it persisted for a day or two, heavily laden rain clouds would fill the sky and burst over the parched earth.

Salah moved on to the subject of drought. He recounted the agonizing march of black slave girls hunting for ants' nests. When encountering such nests, they would squat down and with a quiet, greedy joy fill an old bag with the seeds that had been lovingly gathered by the insects. The task done, the women would triumphantly depart, leaving the anthill in ruins. As for the men, they would hunt the desert iguana for its edible, fleshy tail. They would spend hours watching the entrance to its hole. The iguana always went into the sand head first, so they did not fear the terrible bite of its razor teeth. They plunged an arm down in search of the creature and felt around until they could seize it by the nape of its neck. Then they pulled their prize to the surface, struggling but rendered helpless by a powerful grip. Little grey lizards that hid in soft, sloping sand dunes were also assiduously sought after in periods of drought.

The total absence of rain could be tragic. This elicited Salah's memories of past famines in which camels were reduced to skin and bone, with protruding spines and flaccid humps hanging to one side. They would sluggishly move about, the stronger animals wandering through the camp at night eating straw mats. The she-camels gnawed on the grass harnessing and were unable to provide sufficient milk to satisfy their young. Each day the nomads abandoned possessions that the caravan was unable to convey, sometimes even their tents and traveling bags. But it was difficult to slaughter the beasts on which they so greatly depended. With their livestock gone, the Legouacem, who had neither plantations nor farmland to turn to, were reduced to extreme misery.

Salah spoke of locusts that swarmed in the autumn. One

evening the sky had inexplicably and suddenly grown dark and the last rays of the sun had been transformed from golden to red. Men coming out of their tents had seen tiny spots flying very low, enveloping the camp in the space of a few minutes. The *acrididae* fly north with mechanical regularity. Some of them, separating from the main body, had landed on the ground, hopping awkwardly about the encampment. The children, shrieking with delight, had tried to catch them but the insects invariably got away. Others flew directly into the children, only to find their path of flight abruptly blocked. The men somberly gazed at this endless insect armada. When the herds left their grazing ground myriads of locusts rose up in their path, only to settle a little further on until dislodged again. Trees and tufts of grass were nothing but humming clusters of red. Slaves and herders beat the air and ground with their sticks, stunning the locusts so that they could be forcibly placed within sacks. In the early hours of the morning the men put straw in the trees, which they then set afire to smoke out the insects. Red locusts were quite succulent and the nomads roasted them over hot embers or mixed them with seeds for a real feast.

The conversation continued for some duration until Larcher gave the signal to leave. He refused to make a speech and limited himself to thanking Mantallah for organizing the evening and for the excellence of the dinner. When he reached the colonnaded part of the first floor he invoked Allah's blessings to thank the women who were concealed in the shadows of the court. They in turn responded with loud ululations. Before descending the narrow stairway that led to the door, he stood back to allow Salah to go first. However, the *sheikh* seemed disturbed by the gesture.

"But you are in command," insisted Salah. "It is for you to go first."

"Not at all," replied Larcher. "You are the person most worthy of respect here. I consider myself somewhat your son this evening."

The critical moment came as they reached the end of the patio. Turning around, Larcher saw that a crowd of guests were backed up behind him, listening in the dark. Addressing Salah in a booming voice, he said:

"I hope I shall have the pleasure of seeing you again before you leave Tindouf?"

Salah, who much appreciated this approach, responded:

"But of course. It is customary for me to pay a courtesy visit to your office."

"Please don't go to this trouble. I was delighted to make your acquaintance this evening. You have taught me a great many things about the desert and the nomadic life. I am still a novice in such matters and it would please me to continue our conversation."

"That is my dearest wish," Salah replied.

"Then why don't you come with your son and adviser for lunch at my residence tomorrow? It will be less elaborate than Mantallah's repast but we can share my humble offerings."

Salah, to whom the invitation was completely unexpected, remained speechless for a few moments. Then he replied mechanically:

"It would be a great honor for me and my companions. I accept your kind invitation with pleasure."

On the way back to his residence, Larcher discussed the evening's events with his officers.

"Salah is a clever leader; he said nothing that would jeopardize his position. His language is rich in imagery and highly descriptive. All things considered, the evening proceeded without incident."

"In the camps," de La Renaudie broke in, "this evening will be interpreted as a reconciliation between the Tajakant and the Reguibat. We must recognize Mantallah's skill and Salah's efforts toward mediation with our administration."

"To use the common expression, I think I have enabled him to save face," replied Larcher. "But the most difficult part lies ahead. Tomorrow at noon we must assemble here. Vogel, meet Salah at the gate to the fort."

"Are we going to show him military honors?" Blizzard inquired.

"No," replied Larcher. "He has not accepted the red cape. I shall address him as chief, but I don't want you to present arms so long as he has not accepted the insignia of his office. However, you are to arrange for his passage through the central court and then on to the officers' mess. Time your arrival at the terrace near the palm plantation for twelve-fifteen. Any orderlies and soldiers he encounters will salute him in the ordinary way."

"And if someone comes out of the buildings and wants to kiss his hand?" asked Vogel.

"Let him. After all, he is a religious figure. Decide on the menu as well."

"I would suggest beginning with an omelette. A nomad gave me an ostrich egg this afternoon which still seems fresh."

"Excellent. But will one be enough?"

"With an ostrich egg the cook can make an omelette for twelve people."

"And then?"

"A simple *couscous*, Algerian-style, with some fatty mutton ribs. For desert, dates and some fresh fruit if obtainable."

"Arrange for rugs to be put down and we'll eat sitting on the ground. He's a decent sort of fellow, Salah. I can't ask him to sit on a chair, especially since he's probably never done it in his life."

Larcher returned the officers' salute and entered his spacious mud-walled house with its white-washed walls and high ceilings. The four officers went on their separate ways, chatting. A sudden breath of freshness swept in from the palm trees, and the first large, fat drops of rain plopped softly on the velvet of four *kepis*.

CHAPTER XII

Storms in this part of the Western desert on rare occasions can be quite violent. Throughout the latter part of the night torrential rain had been lashing down on Tindouf and neighboring areas. The *wadi* in the hollow of the palm plantation had become a raging current. Houses with unsound walls had collapsed and terraces where the mortar had been poorly maintained gave way under the weight of the water. At the end of the morning news reached Tindouf of a flood at Wadi Drâa that was sweeping everything before it. An Arab in the eastern region would have lost his life had it not been for the convenient branch of a tree. Even now the sky was the color of ink and held the implicit threat of new downpours.

117

It was twelve noon. In accordance with his orders, Vogel was at the gate of the Fort to greet Salah, who was accompanied by his son, Ahmed, and Hassan, his adviser. As they walked towards the middle of the central court, Salah felt his apprehension pass. Some of the men who saw him stood stock still; others rushed forward and tried to kiss his hand—which Salah hastily withdrew—or the bottom of his robe in token of deep respect. In front of the office, the orderlies rose and saluted him; out on the terrace Larcher and his officers welcomed Salah with the customary words of greeting.

Throughout the meal the conversation centered on the bad weather they were having. Larcher congratulated Salah on his knowledge of the climate. The wind from the south had indeed brought rain and it was expected to last for several days, thereby sparing the country from drought. Salah quoted the Reguibi proverb which says that "all that the rain damages the rain makes right." Water from the sky meant prosperity, plentiful pastures, and camels in good health. It would seem that the coincidence between his own arrival and the coming of the rain was fortuitous. It was a sign that harmony would at last prevail between the French administration and all the Reguibat.

Larcher in turn developed this theme. It was clear, he suggested, that Allah could not be indifferent to the newly established peace and concord among the nomads. He expressed his satisfaction with the meeting in Bersigou that had produced a solution acceptable to everyone concerned.

At the end of the meal, the topic turned to the central issue. Salah sensed that this time it was useless to procrastinate any further. It was time to state his arguments and to penetrate to the heart of the matter. The surroundings were appropriate with only officials, his son, and his adviser in attendance. So it really amounted to a private conversation with Larcher without witnesses. Salah also realized that Larcher was not going to prod him; therefore, he must initiate the first step. After all, he mused, it was only normal since he was the petitioner. He decided to proceed.

"No doubt, Commander, you know why I am here after being absent for six years. I am seeking news of my son, Mahmoud, who has been detained by the French at Colomb-Béchar. If it is permissible I would like to learn what is in store for him."

"I thought as much," replied Larcher, who was puffing slowly on his pipe.

"I am presenting myself as a grieving father. Although I am the spiritual and temporal leader of all the Legouacem and more particularly the Sidi Allal, my coming should be considered a private matter. As the proverb goes, 'Intention is the sister of action.' "

"I understand," said Larcher simply.

"The guise I assume today as petitioner is not a role I am accustomed to. But out of love for my son, who is close to my heart, I am prepared to accede to all the administration's demands providing they would not pose too great a humiliation. Respect must be paid to my age, position, and title."

The allusion to the *burnoose* was clear. Larcher decided to ignore it and to carry on as if he had not understood. He felt that Salah had advanced a long way on the chessboard. Now it was time that he move his pieces.

"I don't agree with you altogether on your presentation of the facts. Without a doubt you have journeyed long, as any loving father would, and I empathize totally with your predicament. But you are a person of great repute, the most important of all the Legouacem. So, in the eyes of your people, you have come to see the French commander who is responsible for the administration of this country. There can be no such thing as a private action for a man of your rank; anything you do becomes an official statement. Am I wrong?"

"You're absolutely right, but if I may be frank with you, it is precisely this situation that I find so tedious."

"Why?"

"To give you a proper explanation, we must recount the origin of the dispute. I would have sworn on the Koran that I would never meet with one of you. My advisers dissuaded me, and rightly so. But you must imagine my state of mind when the French came into this country twenty years ago."

"I fail to see the basis for your hostility."

"Yet it is quite understandable. For us your coming was an invasion of unbelievers on Islamic soil. However, with time I came to recognize that your presence has actually proven to be beneficial. You interceded in tribal wars and ended caravan raids, and pillaging as well. In doing so you brought peace to Moslems who were tearing each other apart. I am a man of peace and I always vigorously resisted the thought of fighting other Moslems. Tranquility is now at hand and I must confess that we are all very grateful to you."

"If that is so," Larcher exclaimed, feigning surprise, "then why this animosity towards us? We have always held the Reguibat in the highest regard. Furthermore, we served as intermediaries between rival tribes without ever imposing our will upon the native peoples. We have never imprisoned anyone. Especially since there aren't any jails. There is one small room without windows which is intended primarily for soldiers who have committed a serious wrong. But as the *mehariste* units are generally well disciplined, the room is never used. When your son was arrested, I didn't have a place to put him, so he slept in the apartment of one of my offices until he was transferred to Colomb-Béchar."

"We share your sentiments. Your guidance is exceedingly mild, at times too much so. We bear no complaint concerning this matter. Our grievances pertain solely to the nature of your administration and its philosophy. I'm not offering censure, Commander, since you are the first French administrator to receive me with friendship."

"Please elaborate further," Larcher replied.

"I will. You act as though you respect our religion, in its outward manifestations. You avoid disturbing us when we are at prayers and you allow your soldiers to freely practice their religion. You subsidize the repair of our mosques and you even pay for pilgrimages to the holy places of Islam for prominent citizens. But in some respects you do interfere in our religion and customs."

"That's a serious accusation," said Larcher. "Can you offer supportive evidence?"

"You have extended your principles of liberty, equality, and fraternity. You have put subservient tribes such as the Sellam and the Foqra on an equal footing with their masters. It would have been unthinkable twenty years ago for a low-born Sellam to insult the son of the most important leader of the Reguibat with such contempt and audacity! My son justifiably killed an unarmed man in cold blood at close range. Had he not done so I would have died in shame. He washed the honor of the Sidi Allal in blood. You see where France's error has brought us? Do you think that without your presence the Sellam, who have refused to pay us tribute in recent years, would have shown such impudence? It is the French who set the scenario for my son's deed and I hold you directly responsible."

When involved in discourse dear to his heart, Salah neglected all prudence. His expression, which had previously been compassionate and gentle, hardened and his lips narrowed to a bitter line. Larcher preferred not to answer because he wanted to hear the rest. In the midst of the silence, Salah continued:

"The second thing I reproach you for is having deliberately destabilized nomad society—always in the name of your egalitarian principles. I refer to slavery. Why did you free the slaves and close down the markets where they could be bought? By what right do you go against the precepts of our religion and the Holy Koran? Slaves are ours by right; they belong to us just as our herds and our clothes. You should intervene if they are mistreated by their masters—this I grant you. However, when you do everything in your power to free them from our control—this I cannot understand. Their freedom is a great injustice in our society, causing frustration and bitterness among the people. We use slaves to tend to our herds and to milk the she-camels. Their removal is akin to severing our hands, thereby crippling us. An unpleasant situation has resulted in which the slaves, having found a sympathetic ear among the authorities, interpret the law according to their needs. In turn, they let the animals stray and dictate conditions to their masters, who have now become the slaves. It is shameful and scandalous."

Salah seemed to have thrown caution to the winds. But Larcher, who continued to puff slowly on his pipe, still did not answer. The old *sheikh* breathed deeply for a moment or two, took a sip of tea, and more moderately continued his monologue:

"Lastly, our third complaint is your interference in our judicial affairs. Thus far, you have respected our Moslem laws, which are an integral part of our life. The administration has shown respect of our ways, as in the instance of the judgment by the Council of Forty. Yet all of a sudden, in the case involving my son Mahmoud, you disregarded our law and chose to invoke your own judicial system. Is it an equitable arrangement to hold your assize court on soil foreign to our people and without our attendance? What is there in common between my son, who is a Reguibi, and an Algerian Arab or a Frenchman from Europe? Nothing. No, Commander, contrary to your assertion, Tindouf is not France. We are different from you, living in different countries with different languages. Let us each respect the other's customs and motherland."

Salah had finished his tirade. Had he gone too far in expounding this criticism of the occupying power when for the first time in his life a French official had received him as a friend in his own house? He had spoken the truth out of a sense of duty before those who were worthy of his respect. Although his acquaintanceship with Larcher had lasted a short twenty-four hours, he was sure the Frenchman belonged to the category of great leaders who knew how to listen and make decisions. He had not intended to be offensive but rather to speak frankly and clear the air. Whatever might transpire, he was satisfied and relieved despite a nagging sense of uncertainty. He started to speak again in a more conciliatory tone of voice.

"It is perhaps regrettable that I should have allowed myself to say such unpleasant things about your administration. You understand, I do not hold you responsible; on the contrary, I appreciate the warmth of your hospitality. If I have offended you, please forgive me, I beg you, and forget what I have just said."

Larcher smiled and set down his pipe on the edge of the ash tray. He replied very calmly:

"I'm not going to teach you the Arab proverb that 'the stone in the hand of a friend is an apple.' I let you speak your mind because I did not feel I was being personally attacked. Your remarks were quite general but revealing in that I may better understand your steadfast attitude toward us. Perhaps many errors might have been avoided if you had spoken earlier of your true feelings without remaining silent for these six years. Perhaps Mahmoud would have been at your side now. If you had instead cooperated with the French administration in a loyal and honorable manner, the Sellam might never have taken any aggressive initiatives. They have taken advantage of our mutual misunderstanding by attempting to usurp the enviable position your tribe has long enjoyed. By remaining aloof, you have played into their hands and contributed to your own misfortune."

Salah was stupefied. He had never considered such possibilities. He opened and closed his mouth, swallowing hard. Larcher continued.

"Let's reconsider the charges you have made. As we both know, France brought peace to the area. That is one positive point. But France cannot maintain separate sets of laws for different geographical sectors. In all the areas under her control the same laws apply. France holds all men on earth to be equal, despite a past history in which our noble classes held lowlier men in sway. But this is from a distant age and your way of thinking is anachronistic. I am sure that your son and grandson do not distinguish between base and noble, between Sellam and Sidi Allal. Neither you nor I can do anything to reverse this natural evolution. However, the administration has never questioned the laws of vassalage and has never opposed your collection of taxes from subservient tribes.

"Now in regard to your second point, the question of slavery. Since we believe that all men are free and equal, why should we admit that some men because they are black should be exploited by others whom God made white? It's not possible. France too has known slavery, but has abolished it. Few nations in the world still continue the practice of enslaving their fellow man, even among the Moslem states."

"And yet I know those who apply the letter of the Moslem law and who still have slave markets," Salah interjected.

"Yes, I grant you this, but these states and their disciplines of enslavement will disappear. The process of historical evolution is too strong for you to oppose. Your children already understand the situation. From what I have heard, Mahmoud is perfectly familiar with the work of a herder and doesn't need lessons from anyone on the subject. So he will no longer need slaves to do the work which he does himself with such enthusiasm.

"Nonetheless, I have observed that abolishing slavery has caused problems for a society such as yours because of its abruptness. I recognize that it has had an attendant destabilizing influence. After giving the matter considerable thought I have arrived at what I feel to be a viable solution. The former slaves will be very attached to their masters, who have generally treated them well; many are too old to change their way of life and so they will remain in your camps of their own free will. There will be no complaints and for this you will have no obligations. But their sons will not be willing to consign themselves to the life of a herder, as their fathers did before them. They will be drawn to the towns, only to leave the herds unattended. To correct this situation, I therefore propose to give them a financial interest in the profits of the herds. In other words, to remunerate them provided they continue to serve their masters for three years. At the end of this period, the 'work contract,' which would be registered with the administration, would be renewable under the same conditions. What do you think?"

"To be perfectly frank," Salah replied, "I don't agree with your concepts. I could never wholeheartedly endorse the kind of proposal you are making. Your reasoning is that of a rationalist, while I am a believer. Slavery among our people is a right, and we don't have to take equality into account. The Koran provides for it. When I buy a slave I am merely following Islamic law and behaving as a good Moslem. I do, however, recognize that there is an irreversible tide in changing customs. Take Tindouf, for example. Half the people here are former slaves whose standard of living is sometimes higher than that of their former masters. They are laborers, employed on construction work financed by the administration—stone workers, drivers, butchers' boys, shopkeepers, and sometimes even soldiers. So, if you want to stop that exodus to the towns by putting into effect your 'work contract,' I shall do nothing to promote or hinder it. It might be a last resort to save our herds from being abandoned. At least you are willing to empathize with our grievances, a fact that I am cognizant of."

"Now," continued Larcher, "I come to the third point you made, about judicial affairs. We have always tolerated, even encouraged, the practice of customary law. Why then should there be an exception in the case of your son? Because this time the murder was so serious, given the rank of the man who committed it and his victim, the administration was concerned that it would trigger a civil war between two major tribes. Our subsequent decision was based on the desire to maintain peace, and for this reason we have determined that Mahmoud be tried under French law in a region removed from Reguibat possessions. I think you should know that France is adamant on this. But I can assure you that, had the country's security not been threatened, we would never have resorted to French law because we respect your religion and your customs."

Larcher was not too happy with the way he had stated his position, but he thought that the rather peremptory tone he had adopted would perhaps mask to some extent the weakness of his argument. He went on.

"I had assumed, by the way, that you had fully understood my intentions. I noted how skillfully you succeeded in saving your prestige at Bersigou and how you avoided paying the price of blood."

"Yes, I took advantage of the circumstances. In other words, in Mahmoud's absence I protected my interests to the best of my ability, a situation that was not easily defensible. I have to thank you for notifying me prior to Mahmoud's arrest. Your warning was very valuable, for I was able to take the necessary steps for the camp and thwart any impulse the Sellam might have had to attack. I'm very grateful. As far as Mahmoud is concerned, may I have news of him? I'd like to learn what the administration intends to do."

"Your son is being well treated. He is being kept under the gentlest of conditions. Mahmoud is a person of good character and causes no problems. I imagine that he will be tried at the start of the summer, his sentence to be determined afterwards."

"Do you think there will be any benefit derived from the extenuating circumstances, such as his early release?"

"I have no idea about that, but it is common knowledge that

General Pignon will be personally taking care of the case. He is anxious to reconcile our differences with you on the condition that we embark upon a trustful relationship."

Salah understood that Larcher could go no further. Larcher had made it clear that his son's case would be examined in a political light. Salah decided to make the next move. And so he began:

"Commander, I have listened carefully to your attempts at vindicating the administration of my charges. I didn't find your arguments totally convincing, but some of them positively astounded me. I realize now that I was in error by delaying any contact with the French administration. By these actions I lost control over my tribe. Today I have taken the first step. In time I shall find it necessary to proceed further. Tomorrow my adviser Hassan will bring to your office the arrears of taxes owed by my tribe."

"Thank you," Larcher said. "Would you be willing to meet with General Pignon on Reguibat territory?"

"Yes, why not?"

"That being the case, I will send one of my officers to you this summer. Vogel—you know him already. He will tour the camps and will consult with you as to the date of the next meeting in which all the tribes will participate."

"That's a good idea. I am at your disposal. I should like you to talk to General Pignon on my behalf to ascertain the date of my son's expeditious return."

"We'll do our best, I can assure you."

Salah thanked him and got up with difficulty, his legs stiff from several hours of sitting. On the terrace outside he suddenly took Larcher by the arm.

"I do believe in all honesty that we can work out an acceptable arrangement. You see, I am no longer among those who reject France. The implications are obvious. If France left, another administration would take over, probably Moslem. But there would be no guarantee that this would be a better administration. There are Moslems who drink alcohol, do not pray, betray their trust, and exploit others. I respect you, who are Christian, just as I respect Jesus, whom we consider an admirable prophet who sacrificed himself for other men. By the same token we have the deepest respect for the Virgin Mary, who is highly honored in the Koran. As I often say, can one give freedom to people who already have it? The Reguibat received their independence from God. They are not dependent on France, Algeria, Morocco, or Mauritania. They tend their flocks and herds, forever in search of pasture. They trespass upon no country's demarcations, only traversing their own arbitrary frontiers."

Salah raised his head. The sky opened momentarily to reveal a patch of intense blue, freshly washed by the rain, then it closed again as swollen rain clouds rolled slowly in on the east wind. As they moved across the sky, they caught the last light of the setting sun, which tinted them with hues of purple, indigo, and gold. The symphony of forms and colors left the small group of men in reverie. Salah, visibly moved, turned to Larcher.

"Our ancestor Sid Ahmed Reguibi ascribed to us a timeless image which I now confide to you. He used to say, 'The Reguibat are the sons of the clouds.' The clouds bring the rain that gives us water and enriches the pasture for our camels. We are bound therefore—and this is our only dependence—to follow, obey, and go where they lead us as they spread their gifts over this earth. Do not forget, Commander, the wisdom of this, our greatest ancestor."

CHAPTER XIII

"La-illah-illa-llah." "There is no god but God" was the trailing nasal chant of Zein ould Himed as he let his camel amble leisurely along. The beast's two right legs moved forward together and the whole of the animal's body was thrown across to the left, and then the two left legs would come into action on cue while the whole body would be thrown across to the right. In this way the cameleer would feel no jolts from the shoulders or the back, and his legs would remain relaxed, with only an undulation of the buttocks to mark the regular shift from port to starboard. This swinging, supple gait allowed large distances to be covered at speed and without fatigue, and was particularly appreciated by the nomads for it was comfortable and

lent itself to meditation. Zein was in a good mood at the thought of getting back to his camp after a few hours of riding at this unflagging rhythm. At the end of the meeting at Bersigou, he had been unanimously appointed by the Council of Forty to recover the twenty-one she-camels given to the victim's family by the Sidi Allal. Who could carry out this task better than he, with his good-natured character, his ever-ready amenability, and his perfect knowledge of common law? He saw his efforts rewarded. God had wished it, may his will be done.

"*La-illah-illa-llah.*" Zein automatically repeated the compulsive chant. Starting from a deep bass this time, he continued with a modulated crescendo which ended with a very high note. Life was good. To be sure, his mission was not easy. He had already entered into discussions—to use the term becoming more and more fashionable among his compatriots. Salah had received him with affability and his Sellam origins had in no way hampered his dealings with the *caid* of the Sidi Allal, who recognized his merits. The old chief had, however, brought up certain difficulties. He had suggested that they proceed to some modifications in the payment of his debt. He had proposed a racing camel in place of three four-year-old she-camels, and a piece of cloth against a three-year-old she-camel. There was nothing to be said against such propositions—they were provided for in Koranic law—but it was still necessary that the party on the other side should accept them. For Zein this meant an exhausting shuttling back and forth between the opposing camps, which were several days' ride apart. The Sidi Allal had the intention of dragging things out according to the rules of the game in such a situation. But Zein was confident enough in his know-how and his tact in handling people to be able to find some satisfying compromises.

"*La-illah-illa-llah.*" This time the note started from very high to fall back finally into a quavering deeper register. Zein hoped that this mission would prove lucrative for him. Allah knew how needy he was! Money just slipped through his fingers and he didn't know how to be thrifty. He loved the good time too much, fine tissues and good food. His legendary generosity attracted endless spongers to whom he could refuse nothing. His herd was consequently depleted; he owned three adult camels which were not so young as they once were, only two breeding females with their colts, and one young white three-year-old female. Oh, how he would like to be rich! Not too much, however, for the excess of wealth arouses cupidity and jealousy and attracts the evil eye. But he would have liked to be well off, a bit like his father-in-law and his brother-in-law, whom he scarcely liked but whose business acumen and knack for increasing the family herd he recognized. He knew that he did not have their esteem, and if Mokhtar ould M'Rabet had given him his daughter's hand, it was because Fatimatou had threatened to leave her family should there be a paternal veto. Fearing the scandal, Mokhtar had given in, but grudgingly, for he disapproved of Zein's frivolous and fickle nature. But what could Zein do if he was attractive to women? He loved Fatimatou. She was tall—something rare among the nomads. Due to the miserliness of her father at the time of her puberty, the milk diet she had followed was rather mediocre. As a result, her curves were shapely but not excessive. She had the advantage of long legs, which gave her a haughty bearing, a sizable bust, high and firm, a wide face with prominent cheek-bones, a sensual mouth, and two large eyes as black and deep as those of a gazelle. Fatimatou loved him passionately, but she was jealous. She knew that Zein made quite a hit in the camps he visited, and she had a tendency to credit him with adventures that were all too often imaginary, but what could he do?

"*La-illah-illa-llah*." The musical phrase was drawn out in a plaintive monochord over long minutes. If he were rich, he would take a second wife. To be sure, he would have the greatest of difficulties with Fatimatou, but he chased this prospect from his mind. He wondered if his wife was not satisfied—in a more or less unconscious manner—that he should be poor and unable to afford a second bride-price. Sometimes she encouraged him to spend, although she had been brought up by her father in the greatest austerity. He would have to be on his guard, and have a frank talk with her. But he soon gave up this idea to return to the subject on which he had set his heart. Some time ago he had fallen in love with Minatou of the Lahcen ou Ahmed. How beautiful she was! Where Fatimatou was tall, strong, and aggressive, Minatou was slender, graceful, fragile in appearance. She had a pretty little face with glowing eyes, and spoke with great sweetness. It was a long time ago that he had spotted her. He had had the opportunity of engaging her in conversation, and a current of mutual instinctive attraction had come into being between the two of them. Now Zein wanted to sound out the intentions of this girl he was dreaming of. So, two days ago, he had decided to make a detour by her camp under the pretext of looking for a lost camel.

"*La-illah-illa-llah.*" The rhythm of his chant accelerated suddenly like the pace of a horse that moves from a trot to a gallop. Once he arrived at the Lahcen ou Ahmed, Zein went into the travelers' tent. He had stationed himself near the entrance to spy on the wiles and stratagems of the womenfolk, who, as was their custom, never failed to saunter back and forth every time a visitor was announced. To show off their good physiques, the marriageable girls would waddle past in their black veils shifting from one leg to the other in order to make one believe that their fat hindered them from walking. But, by looking at the ankles of the candidates, the real enthusiast was seldom mistaken about the obesity of these girls. If two or three rolls of fat appeared at the height of the ankle-joint, then the girls became interesting. Even by waddling like a duck, the girl with delicate articulation could never mislead the experienced eye. Zein watched these comings and goings with detachment. He was looking out for the beautiful eyes of Minatou, for whom he had gone this far out of his way—but in vain. In the evening, the young men of the camp had invited him to attend an *Azaouan*—an evening of traditional Moorish music. He had joined them in the hope of meeting the one he loved. Generally, at this kind of gathering, the women are attracted by the music and singing and occupy half of the tent behind the separating veil. As this could easily be lifted up, it was the moment for meetings, flirtations, and the exchange of promises.

"*La-illah-illa-llah.*" Zein had almost closed his mouth to murmur the formula in a deep and muffled voice. The young nomads had thrown themselves into the performance of their musical evening. To put rhythm into the music, they were accompanied by a four-string mandolin, a flat tambourine with a rough sixteen-string lyre on top, and a little cylindrical tambourine carried under the left arm. Their plaintive nasal singing interspersed with breathless syncopation recalled the Portuguese fado or the Andalusian flamenco. According to the tradition, they had begun by an invocation to the Prophet, called by his second name Moustapha for the occasion. The other themes followed according to the immutable canons of Moorish song. Pastures and water were described in lines of seven feet. The rhythm was slow and in a slightly sharp key with high and low notes alternating symmetrically. Then came the evocation of war in lines of twelve to seventeen feet, a long stirring appeal finishing on a fairly long phrase. It recounted the departure of the troops, the farewell to the camp, the exaltation of combat. At this moment the tambourines and all the strings of the lyre came into play. At this passage, some singers seized the opportunity to praise the great Seddoum, the celebrated songster of the Reguibat.

> Seddoum, you who have never committed an error,
> You who are a voice and a trumpet that dominate the others,
> You remind me of the echoes of the voice of David.

With no moment of transition, the singers passed onto a

more lively and modulated rhythm. In nine-foot verse they evoked the poetry of the desert, the swinging walk of the camels, the caravans, the song of pulleys at the wells. Then followed a rather long appeal finishing in a brutal syncopation, taken up once again in alternating lines of five and seven feet. This would lead onto an extremely high-pitched passage during which the singer would block one ear and sing until exhaustion. This was the song of the cameleers telling of the calls from the wells, the cries of the colts, and the challenging questions during meetings—but telling also of thirst and heat and sandstorm. Finally, to close the program, the beauty of woman would be celebrated in six or eight-foot lines with a swift and lively rhythm scattered with quavers and changing tones.

O Girl of Legouacem,
Through you I have loved
The pass of Magacem
And the spur of Tichleh.

I will be your lover;
You are old
But more beautiful
Than a hundred.

Far from you an hour
My sorrow is great;
The tears flow
On my two cheeks.

Her marble-veined mouth,
Her scalloped teeth,
The two are brought together
And my whole being is charmed.

"*La-illah-illa-llah*," sang Zein on a long monochord before coming back to the drift of his thoughts. He had not taken part in the musical program of his companions. He was sad and preoccupied for he had still not caught sight of Minatou. Was she keeping herself behind the separation veil of the tent that trembled with every movement of the women spying on the bustle among the men from behind the folds? With the concert over, he considered whether to recite some poems from the classical epoch—Omayyad or Abbasid poetry, but above all the poetry of the pre-Islamic period, the famous "Moalaqat" of Imrou-l-Qays of Tarafa, the works of Al-Khantha, or of Antara, the chivalric hero. Zein was in fact one of the few Reguibat to know this kind of poetry, which a close relation from the confraternity of the Ma-Al-Alnin of Rio de Oro had taught him. Zein prided himself on this, and he knew that he would have to give a recital that evening if he were to charm his hosts and perhaps Minatou as well.

To check on the presence of the one he loved, he launched into three lines that she knew. In a way, it was a sort of password, a signal to rally and be recognized:

I have written to you, O most beautiful of the beautiful
on a page that the wind has carried off..
How would I be able to catch it,
I who am bereft of wings?

At this moment the veil was raised and he caught sight of the ravishing face of Minatou, who was observing him with a flame in her look. Zein then moved imperceptibly closer to the separation and casually stretched out, supported on his elbow. It was then he felt the soft plump hand of Minatou caressing his fingers. Reassured by the presence of his loved one, he went on with his recitation. He considered that pre-Islamic poems came from a school of poetry that best suited the life of the Reguibat. They celebrated great knightly deeds, honor, pride, hospitality, the great sentiments of love and hate in a desert setting. In them was celebrated the camel and the camp, the

waterholes and the caravan, as well as the evocation of the
beloved. In general, the love-smitten knight arrived at the
camp just after his lady had left:

> Halt you two! Let us weep at the memory of a lady-love
> And of moments spent by the break in the dune....
> Of Khawla on the shale of Thahmad there only remain
> Footprints standing out like the traces of a tattoo on the back
> of a hand.
> It is there that, stopping their mounts beside me,
> My companions told me,
> Go not to perish of sorrow but to harden yourself.

Zein had then gone on to the second part of the recitation, in
which he declaimed extracts taken from various authors. The
lady-love having left, the poet recalls his last meeting:

> Her face is as if clothed in the sun,
> The purity of her skin knows no blemish....
> O mouth, radiant as the marigold,
> Whose contours are clear and pure and well-ordained....
> I draw her to me by the two temples.
> She lets herself come to me, delicate of stature,
> Well-fleshed at the bracelets of her ankles.
> When she turns, her perfume breathes out on me
> A breeze from the east bearing the scent of cloves....
> Throat pretty as a mirror,
> Her neck is a white gazelle.

> Her thick and coal-black hair adorns her back
> Like the impetuous cluster of fruit on a date-tree
> Coiled towards the summit....
> Her waist is delicate as a hollowed rein.
> She wakes, spreading musk over the bed of her siesta,
> Without the need of girding up the little she still wears....
> O how like the virgin ostrich egg
> Ochred whiteness richly seasoned with the purest
> Of protected water....

The audience was listening spellbound to Zein, who had adopted a tone that emphasized the stressed syllables at the end of each line. Cries of admiration broke out all around when he had finished his first part. Then he was silent. Minatou ardently caressed his hand. He was bent right down to the carpet and whispered words of tenderness to her. But she had refused to let herself be kissed, even discreetly, not even with those butterfly kisses that imitate the wings of the insect in their gentleness brushing over the skin. Zein had suggested they meet at the end of the evening in the hollow of the dune just outside the camp, pointing out that since she was divorced she was answerable to no one. She had replied with neither yes nor no but simply smiled to herself and asked him to recite some more. From memory Zein recited a fragment of the "Moalaqat" of Tarafa, devoted to the noble she-camel:

Stud mare with sturdy flesh parts
She trots like the ostrich....
She challenges the purest thoroughbred to race
Her legs pursuing each other on the vanquished track....

The masonry of her backbone is a succession of vaulted arches.
The deeps of her neck fit snug in her breast.
Under her haunches is like a den in a thicket, full of game.
Her ribs curve down under the mighty ridge of spine.
Her hocks are powerfully set off from each other like two buckets in the arms of a sturdy sinker of wells....
Such is my she-camel, with her short russet beard and hardy back,
Long striding behind, fast pacing before....

Entranced by the beauty of the lines, the listeners begged Zein to continue. He let them insist for a while and then went on to quote the end of a poem dealing with death by Tarafa Ibn Al Abd:

Once I am dead, make my funeral ceremony measure up to my
life.
Thou, daughter of Maabad, shred your robe for me,
do not degrade me to the level of a man
whose aspirations are less high than mine....
Time and the days will uncover to you what you do not know
And bring to you the news you did not have,
And bring you news more surely still
will be to whom you neither gave
coat for the journey nor a time and place
to come again together....

Spellbound, the people in the tent uttered cries of admiration. Zein was stretched out on the rush mat, his face just
opposite that of Minatou, who was weeping tears of ecstasy
and now let herself steal a few kisses. She had not wanted to go
so far. He asked her if she loved him. Of course she did,
couldn't he see for himself? She was afraid of loving him too
much. At this, Zein murmured into her ear the lines of
Imrou-l-Qays:

What leads you astray from me is that I should die of loving you
and my heart obey all your commands
and that you should have split this heart asunder,
one half killed, the other fettered in irons,
And that your eyes moisten only to plant their two arrows
in the fragments of a slain heart....

"*La-illah-illa-llah.*" At the evocation of his memories, the
musical phrase grew more ardent and piercing, to finish on a
guttural note. They had stayed like that throughout the night,
stretched side by side in the midst of all the others, looking
deep in each other's eyes as they exchanged a few scant caresses
and light kisses, whispering words of love. They had separated
in the early hours, heads empty and bodies afire. Minatou had
held out. She certainly wanted to be Zein's second wife, but

refused to be his mistress or a passing affair. Calculatingly, she thought that, if she could make herself desired and yet resist his passion, she would force Zein to marry her. As he had pleaded his excessive poverty in excuse, she reassured him on this point. She was divorced, and would not be too expensive. For her first marriage, the bride-price had come to a hundred she-camels—but she was a virgin and sixteen years old. All that was different now, and she was going on thirty. For fifteen she-camels, Zein would certainly be able to obtain the consent of her father. Moreover, she was prepared to do without the bride-price and follow him forthwith at the risk of being on bad terms with her family—but only on condition that he should marry her legally. Could he do it? He was not sure and voiced his doubts quite frankly. On no account did he wish to separate from Fatimatou—the mother of his two children, Mohammed and Zeinab, aged four and three. And, if he knew Fatimatou, she would never live under the same roof with another legitimate wife, although the Koran permitted it. To be sure, according to the law he had a free hand to impose this situation—but it would be at the cost of an implacable open war that would bring countless worries.

It was at this point in his musings that he spotted the camp one or two kilometers away. He quickened his pace. Life was beautiful, but how complicated too. His preoccupations abruptly deserted him and he found himself totally happy at the idea of regaining the comfort of his tent and his children, his wife, and his old habits after three weeks of absence and nonstop traveling.

CHAPTER XIV

Zein had his mount kneel a few meters from the tent and began to take off the saddle. He was surprised to see his home closed off by the interior veil which was unfolded and hanging to the ground all the way along its length. His children had not come to meet him as they usually did each time he returned. As he continued to unload his equipment, he made out stifled laughter behind the veil, but not a soul in sight. Fatimatou did not appear proud and joyful on the threshold to wish him welcome. He finished unloading his traveling bags and set the beast free by giving it a light kick in the ribs. The camel got up groaning and slowly made its way to pasture, hesitantly, now and then snatching at a grassy tuft with greedy lips. Zein then saw his father-in-law and his brother-in-law arrive amidst frowns and dark looks. Having no particular liking for them he gratified them with a rather off-hand greeting, to which they only gave a forced response. When he asked them if some misfortune had not happened during his absence, they reassured him but remained enigmatic as to the real cause of his wife's attitude.

Carrying his bags in both arms, Zein began to approach his tent. Hardly had he taken a step when the brassy voice of his wife made itself heard from behind the lowered drapes.

"Stay where you are, don't come another step further. I, Fatimatou Bint Mokhtar, your wife—in the presence of witnesses I forbid you to enter the conjugal tent. Should you refuse to comply, I shall bring the tent down."

Dumbfounded, Zein stopped and asked in a toneless voice: "May I know the reasons for this reception?"

"Certainly. It's very simple. I am a scorned woman. Two days ago, in the camp of the Lahcen ou Ahmed, with your barefaced impudence you paid court to a divorced woman. No doubt you slept with her. Everyone here knows all about it."

"Since when do women order men about? What I did the day before yesterday is none of your business. It's my private life. I wasn't unfaithful to you and I didn't sleep with this woman. We just talked. So stop this stupid circus. You're making a fool of yourself. Open the tent, send away your lady friends, and free my children, whom you have prevented from coming to greet me."

"Never, not until you promise to make amends in public before the whole camp. If you wish to see either me or your children again, I urge you to offer a *targuiba* in the form of an animal to be sacrificed."

Zein's anger was growing and he felt caught in a trap. He could see his father-in-law and his brother-in-law crouched a few meters away, their faces turned towards the ground, their shoulders rising at regular intervals and shaken by silent laughter. He was the laughing-stock of the camp.

Camel sacrificed for the guest of honor

"I don't see why I shouldn't be able to marry a second wife and impose her on you. The Prophet—may Allah grant him salvation and His blessings—permits us this."

"Feel free to marry a second wife, you're so rich," said Fatimatou banteringly. "But I warn you, it will be her or me. I won't live under the same roof with her for a minute."

"And if I were to ask three times to see the back of you, according to the formula in our law—that is, if I were to divorce you on the spot?"

"Why not?" replied Fatimatou arrogantly. "I won't even insist on that! I'll leave the tent at once, with the children that I have in my care because of their youth." And, to the laughter of her friends, she added treacherously:

"Of course, when I do you'll complete the bride-price to my father here which you have only paid a symbolic part of so far. Don't forget that you married me as a virgin and on these grounds you still owe a hundred she-camels."

Highly delighted with these sharp answers, the women manifested their solidarity with prolonged hurrahs. Zein found his wife's argument conclusive and thought it more worth his while to offer a camel than to continue this comedy that was so humiliating for him. So he declared in an oratorical tone:

"Ah, what an age we are living in? The women command and the men obey. May Allah be my witness. I am a poor husband, honest and upright, the victim of the demands and jealousy of his wife. Since you are the mother of my children, I will not repudiate you this time. To show everyone here that I am a man of honor, I'm going to the herd right now to find a camel to sacrifice."

"That's the best you can do," replied Fatimatou in a triumphant voice. "But let's get one thing straight. It's not just any old animal, but a white she-camel I'm talking about."

"Come on, you're making fun of me." Zein was flabbergasted. "It's not serious. Be reasonable. I have only one white camel, three years old. If I sacrifice her, I'll be depriving myself of the possibility of increasing my herd."

"I won't compromise. It's that, or else I'm off—those are my conditions. Take it or leave it. I want a white she-camel and I don't care if it is the only one you have. All you have to do is to squander less on the men, be less of a ladies' man, and think more of your children by becoming more thrifty."

Zein dropped his bags on the ground and went off towards the pasture furious with himself, with his wife, with his father-in-law—who was more than likely at the bottom of this scene, with the women of the camp who had made fun of him—in short, furious with the whole world. How had Fatimatou learned of his talk with Minatou? Probably it was Lemjed ould Aroussi who had spilled the beans! He remembered now the greedy look of that sinister character enviously observing him as he caressed the girl in the tent. He had left before Zein and passed by the camp to inform his father-in-law. It could only be him. Soon, he promised himself, at their next meeting he would take the man on one side with nobody watching and administer a correction he wouldn't forget. Telling such tales was inadmissible. He should have distrusted this man, who wore evil on his face and who was believed to belong to a spell-casting tribe into the bargain. Too taken up with his courting of Minatou, he hadn't made the customary response in such a situation, which is to secure a piece of cloth from the evil person without his noticing. Then he would have burnt it while pronouncing the ritual phrase, "in the Name of Allah the Clement and Merciful..." followed by the name of the person, and in this way ward off the evil spell.

Continuing on his way with long strides, Zein stormed at the new generation of women. Submission to the husband was no longer performed. Never would his mother have given herself up to such an outburst before his father, who moreover had not abstained from cheating on her. It was scandalous. As for Minatou, who knows if her whole act had not been put on in public just to compromise him all the more? What would her attitude be when she learned that he had been obliged to sacrifice a white she-camel to obtain his wife's forgiveness and so be able to return to the conjugal home? Maybe she would despise him. Ah, if only one could do without women! But there it was, such was the weakness of men, they needed women to have children, to put up the tent, and to make love. That's the way things were, unfortunately for men!

He had arrived at the herd and made his way towards the white she-camel. He thought she had an interesting expression. He scratched her neck. The camel moved her lower lip to his face and rubbed his cheek. Her eyes were grave and clear with long lashes. Her coat was smooth and shiny, the sign of good health. He put his mouth close to her ear and asked her forgiveness for what he was going to do to her on account of the stupidity of his wife. He recited to her the lines of a pre-Islamic poem by Tarafa Ibn Al Abd on the beauty of the she-camel. Sighing and with tears in his eyes, he thought how she would have had fine colts and how, with the onset of age, she would have become a magnificently sweet and intelligent beast perfect for carrying the palanquins of women and old people. His heart was sick at the idea of having to butcher such a pure, beautiful, and innocent beast. He cast the blame once again on women in general and his wife in particular and asked Allah to lay waste the tent of that envious Lemjed who was responsible for the whole business. Very gently, he slipped a cord around the neck of the camel, who followed him in complete trust.

In front of the tent, Zein ordered the beast to kneel with a slight whistle and the pressure of his right hand in the hollow of her neck. Submissively, the camel let herself drop to the ground in front, first on her front legs and then with the back, without any of the exasperated groans and grumbles that camels generally utter in these circumstances. He tried to turn her towards the east, in the direction of Mecca, and tied her front legs. Two young adolescents came to lend him a hand. Without any gentleness, they grabbed hold of the camel's head and pulled it down to the right-hand side of the body. Zein unsheathed his long tapering dagger, approached the base of the neck, and with one sharp stroke plunged his blade into the jugular vein while pronouncing the formula "in the name of Allah the Clement and Merciful." The blood burst out in boiling spurts, flooding over the sand and the camel's breast. The camel gave out a heart-rending roar that ended in a hoarse, deep death-rattle. Dreamily Zein wiped his blade on the beast's coat and sheathed it again. He turned towards his tent. His wife was standing on the threshold, her face radiant. She wished him welcome but, still under the double influence of his emotion and fury, Zein did not reply to her. Tall and beautiful, she continued to smile and sent him his children, Mohammed and Zeinab, who threw themselves at their father's legs.

He took them both in his arms, kissed them on the mouth, and brought them up close to the victim that the two young men were now beginning to cut to pieces. The camel's head was stretched out on the ground at the end of the long, lifeless neck, a little to one side and away from the pool of blood that the sand was still absorbing. One on each side of the animal, the two men were stripping the skin off the body using their small pointed knives with precise gestures. The hump appeared, milky white and trembling on its base. It was detached with precision and immediately placed in a large cauldron to be cooked separately. Before it was thrown in the pot full of boiling water Zein cut off two small pieces and gave them to his children as a delicacy. Biting heartily into the fresh raw fat, they ran off towards the center of the camp to show their windfall to their playmates. Once the skin was detached from the animal's body as far as the belly and spread out on either side of the carcass, the men began to use an axe to cut out portions of meat starting from the spinal column. The guts they laid carefully on grassy tufts away from the place of sacrifice. The liver was set to cook alongside the hump in a pot of water on the fire.

With a sullen, frowning air, Zein entered his tent. His wife, who had sent away her friends, had unrolled carpets over the rush mats. The saddle and the travelling bags were already put away. She was burning incense sticks to drive off the stronger smells, and had prepared the tea-tray. Joyfully, she welcomed her husband with all the customary politeness, just as if nothing had happened but with a curious light gleaming in her beautiful gazelle eyes. Conscious of the atmosphere, Zein pretended not to notice the efforts she was putting forth to have herself forgiven.

He was sulking and replied to her words in a forced and artificial way. Fatimatou found the situation rather amusing. She was pleased with her behavior and the flirtatious looks she kept giving her husband were full of promise, but she didn't dare come too close. She offered him the first glass of tea, her knee brushing against his in a well-planned accident. Putting on her little-girl's voice, she inquired about his activities with feigned interest. She asked how he was doing with the retrieval of the Sidi Allal camels destined for the Sellam family, and wanted to hear the news about their mutual friends and various people. At the third glass of tea, an old serving-woman brought in the first pieces of the boiled liver and camel hump. Zein was starving and began to eat, taking alternative bites of liver and fat from the roughly cut lumps that he was holding in each hand. Slightly ashamed after her previous outburst, Fatimatou made herself sweet, attentive, and vivacious. Zein recognized her skill in getting the best out of every situation, and in his heart of hearts he admired her. However, more for fun than from conviction, he had decided to remain reserved. After all, his wife's behavior had been within the norms of custom. Had she perhaps gone too far in demanding the sacrifice of the white camel? It was probably the father-in-law who had prompted his daughter to appear so uncompromising over the flouted family honor.

Night had fallen, but the camp was still full of life. As was the custom, Zein had made sure that a good portion of the meat was delivered to every tent. The voices calling across the dark from around the fires burning in front of each dwelling had the joyful ring of merrymaking. Fatimatou called the children to dinner. She served the family meal on a tray: barley flour cooked in camel fat and a piece of the white camel's breast that she had cooked in the embers. The children enlivened the meal with their jokes and expressions and several times Zein could not repress a smile. Fatimatou's hopes rose. She sent off Mohammed and Zeinab with the suggestion that they should spend the night at their grandfather's, tidied up the tent, and lowered the interior curtain. She lit some fresh sticks of incense and brought a gourd of fresh milk that she offered to her husband. Then, in her most playful voice, she asked him if he had not brought anything back from his journey. More relaxed now, Zein took up his *tasoufra*, the big leather bag decorated with bright colors, and opened its brass padlock with a long key that he carried on a cord hanging round his neck. Without a word, he displayed the glassware, some balls of amber for the hair, a piece of blue material, and a bottle of perfume called "Bourgeois, Soir de Paris." He had bought these presents from a Tekna trader he had met in the north at the Salah ould Ahmed camp. Fatimatou burst out into joyful exclamations. At once she sprinkled herself with the perfume, made as if to hand the amber rings in her hair, and unfolded the material and decided that it would do to make a new dress. Moreover, she was going to try it on right away. Slowly she let her clothes slip down to the floor, watching for her husband's reactions out of the corner of her eye. She was quite naked. Zein admired the harmony of this body which had sufficiently opulent curves for no one to be able to say—as the proverb has it, "He has sand on his knees," referring to those of his companions whose wives were thin. Still seated, he pulled his wife to him with a firm grip and stretched her out on his knees. Fatimatou gave out some little startled cries but let him have his way, and began to undress him while he was caressing her.

Zein ran his hands softly and methodically all over his wife's body, lingering on the firm, heavy breasts and moving down towards the belly smooth as peach-skin. His hands continued down the long, muscled thighs as far as the ankles, then came back up again to stop on her sex—soft as the palm of a hand, according to the lovers' expression. Fatimatou had in fact taken great care to thoroughly depilate this part of her anatomy, as is only proper for a well-brought-up young lady. Zein then moved nearer to kiss her on the mouth, admiring the dark blue of her gums. The color was obtained by rubbing the gums with a powder composed of a mixture of herbal dyes, and the contrast set off the dazzling whiteness of the teeth. Their lips joined in a long kiss and they rolled onto the carpet together carried away by a passion they had long held in. Unbridled cries broke from deep within Fatimatou's throat and she uttered incoherent words of love as the waves of desire shook her loins. Zein worked her body, ceaselessly kissing the base of her neck and her breasts and shoulders.

They continued like this for over an hour. They finished breathless, exhausted, ecstatic. Purring like a cat, Fatimatou came and rubbed herself against him. She admired his eyes and asked him laughingly if his mother had not committed adultery with a Christian to have given him eyes of such a clear and tender blue. Zein said he had no idea. But, on the other hand, he was more or less convinced that her mother must have made love with the devil himself to have produced such an aggressive and difficult girl. She laughed wholeheartedly, but she was worried about a shadow of melancholy that had covered his face for a fraction of a second. Perhaps he was thinking about the other one, the young divorced woman he seemed to be smitten with? Zein reassured her and told her quite frankly that his sadness was due to the death of his beautiful she-camel that he had been obliged to sacrifice so stupidly just to please her. Fatimatou smiled. There indeed was the answer of the man she loved, she thought. Her mind at ease, she drowsed off in the hollow of his shoulder.

CHAPTER XV

The sun was already high when Zein woke. He had not even heard the morning call to prayer. He had spent a sleepless night with Fatimatou, whose passion for him meant repeated and exhausting embraces throughout the night after each one of his absences. In short, it wasn't until the early hours that he had plunged into a deep and refreshing sleep, from which he had only just woken. The tent was empty. His wife had been thoughtful enough to keep away the goats and the children to let him rest. He raised the interior curtain and saw her—as he expected—sauntering about the camp. Zein smiled at the sight. Fatimatou was going from tent to tent under various pretexts to show off the brand new material of her new dress,

151

swinging her hips in a lascivious and provocative way. She was sighing and dragging out her words, exaggerating her tiredness to make it clear to the other wives that even if her husband was fickle, he still loved and cared for her a great deal.

Zein pulled the copper tray over to him and set about making his tea. While waiting for the water to boil, he drank down a long draught of whey that Fatimatou had set in a corner of the tent especially for him. This night of love had put him in a good mood and, being of a practical turn of mind, he had decided to forget the sacrifice of his young she-camel. With a little luck, if he managed to carry out his mission successfully he could hope to get at least one breeding camel out of it for his good offices. As for this marriage, it was more advisable to abandon any idea of taking Minatou as his second wife. Fatimatou was too possessive and too loving to allow him this—and Zein did not wish to complicate his existence. He nevertheless hoped to be able to take his revenge on his father-in-law, who had been at the bottom of his wife's intransigence.

A dog barked insistently at the other end of the camp. Zein looked up and made out three camel-riders on the point of dismounting from their kneeling camels just on the outskirts of the tent, as politeness requires. He put both hands over his eyes to try and make out the faces of the new arrivals, scrutinizing them attentively. He recognized Lieutenant Vogel, dressed as a nomad and without his peaked cap, along with Ahmed ould Salah and Hassan ould Bouali, the son and the adviser of old Salah. Zein let out an exclamation of joy. He had a great deal of friendship for Vogel and appreciated the company of Ahmed and Hassan. The latter he considered to have a fine mind, and he enjoyed his qualities as a negotiator. Nevertheless, he decided not to move. It was his father-in-law's job to welcome new arrivals, and Zein already knew that his father-in-law would be coming to ask his advice.

He was not mistaken. He saw his father-in-law and his

brother-in-law arrive almost at a run, and they asked him breathlessly:

"Do you know who these newcomers are?"

"Yes," replied Zein laconically, in no haste.

"Who?"

"It's the Lieutenant Interpreter accompanied by the elder son of Salah ould Ahmed and his adviser."

"In other words," admitted Mokhtar, "some fairly important people."

"Very important. In any case, the law of hospitality is sacred as far as I know. Father, set up the guest tent straightaway and go and welcome them."

"Yes, of course. But do you think it is proper for me to sacrifice an animal? Thanks to yesterday's camel, we don't lack for meat and so we can do without that ceremony."

"That's not my opinion," said Zein sententiously. "You have the representative of the French Government and the elder son of the chief of the Reguibat confederation at your door. They know the time-honored customs. It's not a question of whether you have meat or not. The sacrifice has its symbolic value. It must be celebrated before the guest of honor to show the esteem in which one holds him. It seems difficult to me, Father, to avoid this custom."

"In that case," replied Mokhtar with growing embarrassment, "I think a young camel will do the job."

"Certainly not. It would be humiliating for our guests and they would not fail to notice that they have been received on the cheap by the Sellam. What must be done," added Zein, looking his father straight in the eyes, "is to sacrifice a four-year-old she-camel—and a white one at that."

"Out of the question!" replied Mokhtar hastily.

"In that case, I shall find myself obliged to remain aloof from you and to let our guests understand that you have failed to observe the elementary laws of hospitality. May I point out, father, that if I had not sacrificed my only white she-camel for the sake of your daughter just yesterday, I would certainly have done so today—and with pleasure. But it's too late, and now it's up to you to act according to your responsibilities."

Without another word, Mokhtar ould M'Rabet left furiously, followed by his son, to go and meet the visitors. Zein let out a great guffaw. His wife had just come back from her stroll through the camp, and he let her in on the joke by telling her how he had taken his revenge on her father. Fatimatou, too, broke into helpless laughter. She knew her father was rich and stingy, and Zein's story had overjoyed her. They kissed. Zein changed his clothes and walked off to greet the newcomers. Women were already bustling about putting up the guest tent far from the stinking animal pen.

Vogel and his companions were pleased to see Zein and they greeted each other warmly. As had been agreed with Salah ould Ahmed during his visit to Tindouf two months previously, Larcher had sent Vogel on a tour of the camps in order to try to set up a major gathering of the Reguibat chiefs who were likely to welcome General Pignon. The situation had become clear. The Bersigou meeting had allowed Salah ould Ahmed to avoid paying the blood money and to reinforce his prestige while at the same time satisfying the victim's family. Hamoudi ould Himdoun, the *caid* of the Sellam, had also succeeded in bringing off a public relations coup that gave him greater credibility with his turbulent tribe. Salah ould Ahmed had come to Tindouf and a real dialogue had been set up between himself and Larcher that had brought the grievances of the litigants back into a more realistic perspective. Finally convinced that he had made an error in maintaining a policy of abstention, Salah was now disposed to work with France. In short, by taking things step by step and dealing tactfully with the susceptibilities of everyone concerned, Larcher had managed to re-establish the situation.

The most difficult step was yet to be achieved—the handing

Departure of patrol from Ain Ben Tili to Iguidi.

over of the *burnoose* to Salah in the presence of the chiefs of all the tribes before the assembled troops. There was no question of sending out a general without getting something in compensation. Conscious of the honor to be done him, Salah would evidently have to give some pledge of good faith in return. Vogel was confident, convinced that Salah was ready for any sacrifice in order to get back his son. It was necessary to show him that the ceremony of investiture was going to reinforce his authority and not diminish it, elevate him in the eyes of the confederation and not humiliate him.

Vogel had been dropped off at Ain Ben Tili, where his two companions Ahmed and Hassan were waiting with a splendid *azouzel* camel for the journey. Travel at this time of the year was particularly trying, for the heat in June is generally intense. Awake at dawn, the three men mounted their beasts and at a leisurely pace rode without a halt until midday. They arranged to drink in the saddle every hour because they were so parched, but it was just a few sips of brackish water tasting strongly of tar and squeezed out of the goat-skin bottles fixed to their saddles. At noon, they halted and hastily set up a shelter composed of a simple tent cloth supported on two sticks and two guns vertically, butt down on the sand. They crouched in this precarious shade to eat a handful of crushed dates, and even contrived to drink some scalding tea. Freed of the saddles and equipment, the camels lay flat out on the ground without the strength even to get up and eat the few plants which had still managed to resist the sun at this time of year. Around three in the afternoon, the small group set off again until nightfall. Then the three men freed the camels and gathered up wood to cook their meager cameleer's fare, noodles with tomato sauce and tea. Then, with stiff legs and aching backs, they collapsed onto their sheepskins to recuperate their strength in a deep, refreshing sleep.

During the journey, Vogel had had the time to work out the details of his tactics with his two companions. He had decided to be completely frank with them, considering it a waste of time to try to pull the wool over the eyes of such intelligent people. His listeners agreed that the circumstances were favorable. By policy rather than by conviction, Salah was prepared to make concessions in the hope of recovering his son. Vogel proposed that Salah himself should set up the meeting with the commander-in-chief of the area—and this would permit him to strengthen his credibility with the tribes. In that case, he would send out invitations approved by the administration. In these convocations, there would be no mention of the official handing over of the *burnoose*, but nothing would prevent the occurrence of such a ceremonial during a short military parade. In exchange, it would doubtless be appropriate to promise Salah the earliest return of his son.

Vogel's listeners found this plan fairly satisfactory. They intended to help the lieutenant wholeheartedly and to work towards a definitive reconciliation of Salah with the administration. To Vogel they voiced their desire to get out of the deadlock in which their leader had placed himself and which had shown itself in the end to be prejudicial to his authority. The Sellam had taken advantage of this to move into areas left vacant. Salah, therefore, had to devote himself to re-establishing his prestige over the entire confederation. With this in mind, it was necessary for the three men to be able to arrive directly at Salah's home. If the latter accepted the proposed plan, they would then be free to make a systematic round of the various camps that were to be involved in the gathering that autumn.

The camels could hold out for four days without drinking, so the little group made swift progress without worrying about a possible detour to find water at a well. Around mid-morning on the fifth day, they saw the conical forms of the tents silhouetted against the foot of the dunes of the *erg iguidi*. The three companions looked at each other with a smile, pleased to have arrived so quickly at their destination after an exhausting journey. The camels sensed the presence of water nearby and quickened their pace to a trot. Indeed they were beginning to suffer from thirst, and the dried-up skin around their bellies made the ribs stand out.

Salah gave Vogel an effusive and friendly welcome. He appeared touched by their visit, carried out in the full heat of summer at a time when even the nomads themselves avoided traveling long distances. On the first day, Vogel rested in the guest tent specially set up for him, which he shared with Ahmed and Hassan. The negotiations with Salah began with either Ahmed or Hassan as intermediary. In the morning, Salah would arrive in the guest tent and make light conversation with Vogel on a variety of subjects for several hours. In the afternoon, it was Vogel's turn to go to Salah's tent and stay there until evening prayer. Thus he was present for the return of the shepherds, who came to make their daily reports to the master, who would sit in the middle of the tent flanked by the principal personalities of the camp on either side.

On the evening of the fifth day, when Vogel was beginning to despair at the lack of progress of the negotiations, his two companions came to announce that Salah had finally agreed to send out the invitations jointly with the administration. During the whole of the following day, Vogel wrote dozens of letters of convocation in Arabic, in the name of Major Larcher, in which he indicated that a gathering had been organized at Ain Ben Tili, to be held at the beginning of the following October in agreement with Salah, chief of the Legouacem. Then he worked out the quickest and most appropriate route to visit the other camps during the thirty days that remained before getting back to Tindouf. Vogel had already carried out about half of this mission when he arrived at Zein's camp.

After the exchange of greetings, Vogel entered the tent that had been set up in record time for the guests. He drank the three glasses of tea to mark his welcome and, as it was still very early in the morning, decided to hear the grievances of the

A complaining man before elders

plaintiffs in the presence of the camp notables. The lieutenant took pleasure in trying to sort out the quarrels that his coming brought to light. As the representative of the administration, he could give a definitive and official character to any solution of a dispute. So, the nomads being idle at this time of year, they sought out his presence as soon as his arrival was known in order to set forth their grievances, some of which dated back several months—not to say years. The whole business was all the more sought after since the litigants were able to mix business with pleasure. They shared the high table of the camp chief and ate the meat of the camel slaughtered for the guests of honor.

The session began with the suit of a rejected husband. In the absence of his wife but with his father-in-law, Said, present, Najem vehemently accused his spouse. Not long married, the wife had "repudiated" her husband—to employ the legal term. Vogel admired the nomad women's faculty for showing their independence—in contrast to their more settled sisters who were more submissive to their husbands. From the embarrassed answers of Said, those present understood that the father was in league with his daughter to force Najem to ask for divorce. Said did not attempt to contradict his son-in-law. He admitted that his daughter listened to nobody—not even her father or mother. But if she refused to follow her husband, was it for this that she had "to be cut into little pieces and burnt"? It was a skillful defense. Impressed by the apparent good faith of the father, the camp elders proposed two very simple solutions: the plaintiff should either divorce his wife, or else he should win her back by setting her up in a new tent, giving her silver bracelets for wrists and ankles, and offering her a *targuiba* in the form of a young she-camel. Then, perhaps, touched by the generosity of her husband, she would consent to return to the conjugal bed. Najem, a pitiful husband in love with his wife, chose the second solution. He promised to set up a new tent for his wife along with the customary gifts in the autumn, "at the time when nature grows green again."

The next affair was more complicated. When Lemen had set out in search of five pregnant camels that had strayed away, he found Kerkeb riding one of them. The latter claimed that two camels had arrived one evening in his camp in the *iguidi*. He had sold one and was making use of the other, but he knew nothing of the other three. He therefore consented to refund the price of the first, return the second for a slight financial compensation, but on no account would he take responsibility for the other three. The elders were positive: if two out of five pregnant camels had arrived in Kerkeb's camp, then he knew perfectly well where the other three were; she-camels in this condition only move about in groups. Kerkeb dug his heels in, saying that he was ready to take the oath. Vogel did not like this. To be sure, Moslem law said that "proof should be brought by the accused and the oath by the one who denied," but the application of this frequently invoked practice nevertheless remained very rare, since it seemed a very grave step. It was therefore deemed preferable to employ this as a last resort. Moreover, Vogel had the feeling—shared by the audience— that Kerkeb was lying. The three camels were therefore attributed to him, with a deadline of forty days to bring them back to their owner. Faced with this unobliging verdict, Kerkeb stepped down. After much haggling, he agreed to pay the victim three she-camels (each a year and half old), the price of an adult camel in pieces of cloth or in sheep, and the price of a quarter of another camel.

The third dispute concerned the "loan" of camels, which is called *meniha* in Arabic. Under the Reguibat law, this custom consists of receiving in exchange a nanny-goat or she-camel which can be milked during the lactation period, or a camel for ordinary employment whose coat-hair can be utilized—but no more than this. In reality, it is a pact of mutual assistance between rich man and poor. The latter can thus use a few camels as he wishes, and it is up to him to pay the *zekat*—the

The game of *Hib*

religious tax that is one of the five obligations of Islam—in place of the owner. As for the rich man, this practice allows him to make an investment, save on the cost of guarding the animals, and do good at little expense in the hope of "earning the divine reward." The increase in stock by breeding remains the property of the lender, but after a few years he probably does not know the size of his herd, which has increased in the meantime. The disputes which follow are difficult to resolve. However, both the owner and beneficiary try to come to an agreement, the former because he risks losing the benefit of his good deed if he complains too much and the latter because he may incur the wrath and punishment of God if he is dishonest. Vogel did not hide his admiration for this institution based on solidarity and generosity, which allowed the poor to benefit from the wealth of the rich without being humiliated.

The flood of plaintiffs dried up at the moment of the five o'clock prayer. Now was the time of relaxation before sunset. Groups formed in the tent to watch or play checkers on a square of sand. Instead of pawns, one of the players used twigs of wood, the other balls of dried camel dung. Some youngsters in front of the tent undertook to demonstrate their agility in the game of *Hib*. One of them would perch on one leg in the middle of a circle of his playmates, who turned round him; teasing and hitting him with the flat of the hand; he was supposed to touch one of the circle using only his free raised foot. The one who was touched would then take his place, and the game would go on. To avoid the whirling foot, the youngsters leapt about with hoarse guttural cries that were generally reserved for the training of young camels.

General conversation revolved around lost camels. Vivid descriptions of the branding marks, colors, and physical peculiarities of the lost animals were given. News was asked of three pregnant camels; one with a red coat and *qaf*—the distinctive brand of the tribe—on her neck, the second a "young gazelle," and the third a "gray turtle-dove." Two young camels belonging to Mokhtar had been lost, one piebald and the other "smoky" piebald, but both still with their humps. One nomad mentioned that he had found a four-year-old camel in his herd which had an unknown brand done in tar. It doubtless belonged to the Berbers of the Moroccan South. Someone else said he had seen two *mehara* race camels in very good condition with good humps, one grey and the other russet with white breast and foreparts. A grey she-camel had also been spotted. She had white bracelets on her fetters, a white patch on the end of the nose, half the tail white, a ball of skin under the jaw, and the top of the right ear vertically split.

A lively dialogue was struck up between Zein and Chaabane, to the great glee of the listeners.

"If you want to buy a camel in a herd that you don't know, how do you know which is the best?"

"I crouch behind a bush and let my head pop up. I take the first camel to spot me, even if he is ugly, because he's the best for work."

"If *mehara* with different-colored red coats have spent the night traveling, which one arrives first before all the others in the morning?"

"It's the camel with a russet coat, with white breast and foreparts."

"Which camel that has carried a heavy load all day arrives back in the best form?"

"It's the white camel."

"Which camel has the smallest eyes?"

"It's the young unbroken male."

"Which she-camel kneels first in the pen reserved for the herd at night?"

"The camel with a full udder."

"Which camel spends the whole day in the pasture, without her udder-bag being taken off, and arrives in camp in the evening without any milk?"

"It's the carob-tree camel. She eats the carob at the top of the tree, and in so doing she stretches up with all her neck and her body. The young colt has been able to suckle without breaking the udder-bag."

"Which is the first she-camel to be impregnated?"

"The camel that has been helped."

"Which camel always kneels down away from the others when he comes back to the camp in the evening?"

"It's the shy and skittish camel."

"Which camel walks on his hair?"

"The piebald camel."

"Which camel doesn't mix with the other camels?"

"The young stud."

"Which camels go down face to face when they kneel?"

"The young colts."

"If you have a castrated male to which you are accustomed and which has never roared, and it begins to do so, what does this mean?"

"It means he has a premonition about the absence or death of his owner."

"Which camel always defecates in the same place?"

"The camel with his tail cut off."

"Which camel eats only one side of the bush and leaves the other?"

"The one-eyed camel."

At this answer, there was laughter all around. Then they moved on to play the game of rhymes. Each man in turn composed a four-line verse which he recited in answer to that of his fellow. Among these often-illiterate nomads the art of composing verse came easily. They did this for fun and to relax, showing great imagination and an astonishing wit and sense of poetry.

CHAPTER XVI

In the rear-view mirror, it was difficult to see the Dodge six-by-six that should have been following the Land Rover at high speed. The dust from the track rose up in enormous, dense, reddish spirals, stretching over several hundred meters. Larcher slowed down, then stopped, mindful of the rule for two vehicles traveling in the Sahara. His glance slid over his passengers. De La Renaudie leaned against the window of his door, dozing. Brahim ould Kountaoui, the guide, was asleep in the back with his head in his arms. It had been light for scarcely an hour and a chill wind blew under the canvas awning of the hood. Larcher shivered and lit his pipe.

The Major was satisfied. At the end of September, as

166

planned, General Pignon had placed the red *burnoose* on Salah ould Ahmed's shoulders before the Reguibat chiefs assembled at Ain Ben Tili, during an impressive gathering of tents and camels. Having arrived the day before, Pignon and Larcher had not slept that night—for the suspense had indeed lasted until the last minute. Blizzard's camel troop had ridden there to present arms to the general and to the officers and important guests coming from nearby Mauritania to attend the ceremony. The tribal chiefs of Reguibat Sahel had also been invited at the request of Salah, who wanted to give a certain glamor to his reconciliation with the French government.

The guests had taken their places in a row in front of the tents, and the important personalities were presented to Pignon, who managed to call them by name within the first few seconds of conversation without making a single mistake in the sometimes difficult pronunciation of the Arabic names. He inquired about the location of their camps, and asked news of the rain, pastures, and herds, and of the health of the women and children. As he had crisscrossed the region twenty years before when he was a young camel corps lieutenant, he was proud to show the nomads that he knew their country well. The Reguibat were impressed, drinking in his words and uttering exclamations of sincere admiration whenever Pignon pronounced the name of a man or a well or a place with the proper accent. Once in front of Salah, he lingered rather more. He listened carefully to the old chief, giving the impression of showing him special attention. Salah, who was at first on edge but then more relaxed, played along with this game and sprinkled his answers with notes of humor.

Once the presentations were over, Vogel had left the nomad chiefs in their places and brought Salah out of the line to place him in front of the massed troops. Pignon set the red *burnoose* on the old chief's shoulders and pronounced the ritual phrase of investiture. The camel corps presented arms. Proud and dignified, Salah let all this happen without uttering a word.

Pignon had then presented him with a magnificent rifle, a cavalry automatic with a brass plaque on the butt engraved with Salah's name. After thanking him, Salah entrusted the *burnoose* to one of his aides and took the General by the hand, keeping the gun with him. The two men went towards the guest tent followed by all the guests, who were rather thunderstruck by the scene they had just witnessed. They had, in fact, been kept in the dark about the proceedings of the ceremony until the very last minute. For the nomads who had come from Ain Ben Tili, it was a question of receiving the general commanding the territory on Reguibat soil. As Salah was taking part in this welcome for the first time in many years, they had understood that the hour had struck for the reconciliation of the Sidi Allal with the official government. But at no time had they imagined the handing over of the *burnoose*. Inside the tent, the usual speeches were made. Salah intervened in a moderate tone to thank France for having brought peace to the region. Nobody else had dared to take the floor, not even the Sellam. Salah had completely re-established his authority.

Three months after this gathering, Larcher was bringing Mahmoud back to his father. The six-by-six finally appeared with Vogel at the wheel, along with Salah's son and two Arab soldiers. Reassured, Larcher started the engine and pulled away. They had decided to drive fast, for the road was long. He took up his train of thought again. His mission had been accomplished and Pignon, who was not generous with compliments, had congratulated him. He had managed to control the whole of the Legouacem and bring Salah around to better feelings towards the administration. To be sure, this unhoped-for result had been made possible by the imprisonment of Mahmoud in Colomb-Béchar and by his father's desire to obtain the boy's liberation as quickly as possible. The blackmail had, however, been discreet and Salah had not felt humiliated.

And yet, all these efforts had perhaps been deployed in vain, thought Larcher. Morocco had just welcomed back its king on his return from exile in Madagascar, and was going to obtain independence. The Moroccan Liberation Army in the Drâa was beginning to be talked about. Information received made it clear that there was considerable worsening of the nomads' attitude. The Algerian-Moroccan-Mauritanian borders would evidently have to suffer the repercussions of such a development. It took little imagination to foresee that a zone of unrest was going to be created. If the situation got any worse, Larcher would find himself vulnerable. His manpower reserves were ridiculously small to hold the several-hundred-kilometer frontier.

The two passengers woke up, somewhat ashamed to have let themselves drop off to sleep. Larcher, who was the eldest of the three and had been driving tirelessly since morning, scolded them gently. Brahim scrutinized the terrain, then asked the Major to leave the Tindouf-Ain Ben Tili track and head off due south. His directions were given in a vivid manner, the vocabulary being at once precise and picturesque. He had the vehicle head straight for "the red hill," which was at first blurred and indistinct but finally turned out redder than the neighboring heights. He invited Larcher to place the gum-tree—isolated growth in the middle of a pebbly plain—"on his left eyelash" or to head straight for a granite rock by placing it "between his two eyes"; he asked him to execute an erudite turn around a tuft of grass, which suddenly took on momentous importance, a deeply symbolic value, as if the whole world all of a sudden turned on this puny, stunted shrub. Brahim was an excellent guide, and an exception in his profession, for the sureness of his judgment was rarely troubled by the vehicle's rapidity of progress as compared with the steady advance of a camel. When faced with a treacherous, dry, sandy *wadi*, he would indicate the one crossing to use, and his opinion was always right, Larcher was sometimes skeptical aout the proposed route, but after some distance he would realize it was superior

A guide

to the one he would have taken. Prizing his reputation, Brahim would spend hours on end interrogating the nomads in the camps in order to add to his ever-increasing stock of information concerning the nature of the terrain he crossed by day or even by night. For the stars were good guidemarks as they rose one after the other over the horizon. Venus, "the Shepherd's Star," the first to rise and the last to set, and "Belhadi," the Pole Star, were well-known to the Reguibat. Belhadi was the nomads' point of reference; placed between the eyes, it showed North; on the left or right eyelash, northeast and northwest; on the left and right temple, east and west. To head south, the cameleers preferred to use the constellation of Scorpio, recognizable by its bent-back tail, or else the Southern Cross with its slightly squashed parallelogram.

Larcher enjoyed driving off the beaten track. Alert to the directions given by the guide, it was his job to pick out the best surface over which to advance. Any false move by the driver was at once penalized. One had to carry out delicate maneuvers without any hesitation: disengage the drive-wheels, change down gently, accelerate or slow down where necessary. Sandy stretches were the big test. Taken at high speed, if the vehicle happened to get bogged down with the wheels spinning uselessly, the driver's reputation would suffer. Once the vehicle was stuck, a series of exhausting operations was necessary. The axles had to be dug out with a spade or sometimes by hand, lying flat on the stomach under the burning chassis. Then, in order to build up speed, sheets of metal were placed underneath the wheels or, lacking that, bundles of dried grass. The driver then had to move off cautiously and smoothly and without jerks and, once out of the ruts, avoid getting bogged down again.

The sun had hardly set when the two vehicles arrived in sight of Salah ould Ahmed's camp. Knowing the way things should be done in desert life, Larcher decided to stay where he was. "The guest was white," says the proverb. He should arrive in daylight so that the people in the camp had time to prepare his reception. He told Mahmoud to make his way to his father's tent with a message requesting hospitality for the following day at ten o'clock. Drunk with his newfound liberty, Mahmoud put the note in his pocket and left at a run. A few minutes later, distant cheers could be heard and fires were lit in front of the tents to celebrate the return of the prodigal son.

At the agreed hour the next day, the two vehicles started to move at low speed. A kilometer from the camp, some twenty young *meharists* mounted on racing camels surrounded the convoy and escorted it as far as the tents, firing their rifles in the air. Larcher made his way towards Salah, who was flanked by all the elders in a row in front of the tent. The two men gave the ritual embrace. Salah was radiant and declared for all to hear:

"This is one of the finest days of my life. You have returned my beloved son Mahmoud to me alive and well. You have kept your word, and I have kept mine as well. May the blessings of Allah be upon you, and upon all your officers, whom I now take the opportunity of thanking. May harmony, peace, and friendship reign between the Sidi Allal and France."

Before going inside the ceremonial tent, hung with Moroccan long-wool carpets, Salah requested Larcher to show a little patience by attending a *meharist* warrior display. Jumping off their camels, the riders came to perform a mimed dance full of precise gestures. Bent over and walking with little steps as if seeking to drive an imaginary enemy out of cover, they suddenly came face to face and aimed their rifles at each other. At that moment, crouching right down to the ground they threw their rifles high in the air and skillfully caught them again before they fell to earth. This spectacle was accompanied by rhythmic handclapping and cries, and the shouts of the admiring spectators who appreciated the skill involved in catching the rifles whirling in the air like dislocated crosses. After this entertainment, a magnificent white she-camel with clear eyes, measuring two meters to the withers, was brought forth for the sacrifice. Larcher tried to dissuade Salah from slaughtering such a fine beast, but the old chief would not hear of it in view of his joy at recovering his son.

The day was spent in the best of spirits. Salah had had the women work throughout the night and the food was excellent. A *couscous* was served, consisting of grilled barley moistened with rancid butter and pieces of camel breast roasted in the embers. At the end of the afternoon, Salah took Larcher for a walk in the outskirts of the camp to stretch their legs before the sunset prayer. As his host was in excellent humor, Larcher thought it a suitable moment to get down to political matters. He did not need to question Salah, who brought up the current situation himself and inquired about the return to the throne of the Sultan of Morocco. Was France going to give independence to Morocco, as rumor had it? Larcher explained that, after an ill-fated endeavor, his country had resolved to meet the aspirations of the Moroccan people. However, he added, what was good for one country was perhaps not good for another. Here, for example, they were on Algerian—and hence, French soil.

Salah listened attentively to Larcher's explanations, but wondered if it were possible and realistic for France to give independence to Tunisia and Morocco and not to Algeria. For the Reguibat, to be sure, such a notion did not mean much unless it was the transfer from one administration to another. The nomads did not consider themselves to be on Moroccan territory. The nationalists of the Istiqlal party claimed that their country extended from Tangiers to Saint-Louis in Senegal. But that was just an idea without foundation, a subject for propaganda and no more. In the course of centuries, the sultans of Morocco had sent a few expeditions across the Occidental Sahara, and their troops had gone in for proselytizing. Certain kings, such as Moulay Ismail, the grandfather of the present sultan, had carried out a number of incursions in the south of the Drâa and had met up with some of the "Ait Oussa" and the "Tekna" tribes. These apparitions of Moroccan power were, however, ephemeral. So, today, the *marabout* priests of the "Ma Al-Ainin" brotherhood of Rio de Oro considered themselves subjects of the Moroccan kingdom, but not the Reguibat. This being so, concluded Salah, the personality of the sultan, the circumstances of his return to the throne, and the granting of independence by France undoubtedly represented a new focus of interest for the nomads, who could be expected to have a lively feeling of fellowship with the kingdom.

Larcher thanked Salah for his analysis which did not surprise him. He understood that the Reguibat could not remain unmoved by the developments in the north, just at the edge of their traveling limits. Moreover, the South Moroccan localities such as Goulimine were veritable "ports of the Sahara" and vital for the nomads, who could dispose of their camels in the markets there. By chance, the Moroccans were great eaters of camel meat, and sales of herds in the north were assured. Under these conditions, Larcher pointed out, it would be child's play for the Moroccan authorities to recruit into the Moroccan Liberation Army young nomads attracted by the lure of profit and the acquisition of arms. With their knowledge of the terrain, these young men would soon become redoubtable warriors.

Salah protested. For sure, young people these days were difficult to control. But, for himself, he would use all his authority to prevent the recruitment of Reguibat into the Liberation Army. And what was this army for? To combat the French and the Spanish? For what reason? Morocco had obtained its independence within its natural frontiers. What more did it want? The sultan had the agreement of France to recover his throne. Why should he make war indirectly through the tribes? To satisfy imperialist designs and encroach on the territories of Algeria and Morocco? If he considered that the South of the Drâa belonged to him, why not start up negotiations with the French President? Had not the Prophet —May Allah grant him Salvation and His Blessings—said that "arrangement is preferable" to any form of conflict?

Larcher was pleased to hear such ideas but, in spite of the evident sincerity, Salah seemed to him to be singularly naive. He finally asked Salah the key question—the one he had been dying to ask for so long—about his position with regard to an eventual visit to the sultan. Salah showed his surprise. He stopped and looked Larcher in the eyes.

"What do you mean? Me go to Rabat to pay my respects to the King?"

"Yes, that's just it."

"Why not? I've already been thinking of it and I look on this long and tiring journey with favor. I have nothing to do with Morocco and the Moroccans. I am an independent man, as I have already explained to you. But the sultan of Morocco in my eyes represents the highest Islamic spiritual authority. It would be an honor for me, a privilege and a joy, to meet him once before my death."

"You are not unaware, however," replied Larcher, "that by going ahead with such a visit you are making an act of allegiance to the King. As you are Chief of the Confederation of the Legouacem Reguibat, people will say that the Reguibat have become subject of His Majesty."

"Not at all, such an idea never entered my head," replied Salah spiritedly. "I'm going to pay my respects to a spiritual leader, the 'Emir El-Mouminin,' the 'Prince of Believers,' rather like you Christians when you go to visit the Pope in Rome. Do you thereby consider yourselves subjects of the Vatican?"

"It's not the same problem here," pointed out Larcher. "You told me yourself that in Islam temporal and spiritual powers were combined. Your journey to Rabat will be interpreted by all the Reguibat as a gesture of submission to the sultan, even if you think the contrary. You can do nothing against this. Your action will encourage the young Reguibat to enlist in the Moroccan Liberation Army and open fire on our forces under the pretext of returning this territory to Morocco."

Salah stayed speechless a moment. He had never dreamt of such a prospect. Larcher's argument had hit home. Abruptly. he understood the full significance of his act. He started walking again.

"Does this mean that you are going to prevent me from going to the sultan—if, that is, I am entreated to go?"

"How could I?" exclaimed Larcher. "You are free, and as elusive as all the nomads. It's a serious business and it's up to you alone to face your responsibilities. I respect your religious feelings. I also understand that you would wish to see the Prince of Believers before dying. But, in the position you hold, that cannot be done without grave consequences."

"Do you mean by that that the French Administration will hold it against me?"

"Certainly."

"Why? Do you think it a question of treason? Isn't it France that brought the sultan back to the throne?"

"Yes, of course, but it would be a kind of treason all the same, for you belong to an administrative system, which is not that of Morocco. By your action, you would incite the Moroccan nationalists to claim this part of the Sahara that you consider your own. You would add fresh fuel to the propaganda of the Moroccan Liberation Army. Their leaders would be able to say: 'The greatest *caid* of the Reguibat has just paid allegiance to our Sultan. Let us therefore go and "deliver" our brothers still under the yoke of French colonialism.' The frontier would be closed and you would be cut off from your family."

Larcher took a breath and maintained his impetus: "It would be a pity—just when you have regained control of the whole of the Legouacem thanks to your cooperation with us, now that you at last have your hereditary enemies, the Sellam, at your mercy—it would be a pity to compromise all these results."

"I thank you for your words of friendship," put in Salah. "Before making such a decision, I shall think twice."

The two men had finished their walk and returned to the camp, in silence, immersed in their thoughts. The sun was setting on the horizon, an immense red disk. It was the hour when the flocks came back from pasture, hurried along as well as possible by the bustling shepherds running barefoot in the dust. A concert of bleats, barks, and cries rose from the camp, silent until then under the heat of the day. The animals stood out like shadow puppets against the violent sky as it was gradually overtaken by the night. Awkward and hesitant, the camels offered scarcely any resistance to entering the enclosure set off by its rough hedge of thorny branches. The goats, by contrast, scattered around disobediently with their young. Some of the bolder kids ended up climbing on the tents and sliding down with their four legs in the air like children on a slide. It was a comic sight, and the two men exchanged a smile of complicity.

"I hate politics," said Salah. "Why spoil this twilight peace with ill-timed and out-of-place reflections? Let us seize our joy. Nothing will happen to come between our friendship."

"I truly hope so," replied Larcher, "and such is my dearest wish. But everything depends on you."

"Yes, on me, but also on Allah whose designs are inscrutable."

Salah excused himself and, obeying the last call of the *muezzin* as it rose into the pure air, went to take his place in front of his men to lead the prayer at sunset with all his customary dignity.

Larcher found the guest tent empty. He rounded up his two officers and swiftly related his conversation with Salah.

"We are paying for the humiliation of the *burnoose*," commented de La Renaudie.

"That has nothing to do with it," replied Larcher. "Salah does not hold that against us, just the opposite. He thinks he has regained control of his tribe by this means. We are paying for the Sultan's return to the throne. What can we do against that? How can we make the nomads understand the subtlety of our policy?"

"I agree with your analysis," put in Vogel. "I've had a long discussion with Ahmed, the elder son of Salah. He has become a real friend and has 'opened his heart to me,' to use the stock phrase. Salah has already been approached by the tribal chiefs, who have urged him to go to Morocco to make his act of allegiance to the Sultan. He has neither agreed nor refused. He was probably waiting for the return of his son Mahmoud. But, according to rumors, Moulay Mehdi himself is halfway to persuading Salah to go to Rabat."

"This information confirms the impression I got from my conversation with Salah. He's slipped away from us. My arguments will carry little weight against those that will be brought up by Moulay Mehdi, who is his father-in-law and has an undeniable moral influence over him."

A heavy silence settled over the three officers, troubled only by the murmur of the men finishing their prayer just a short distance away. Larcher suddenly had the impression that a new era was beginning, an era of violence, blood, and tears. War was inevitable, along with its cortege of the suffering. Were they going to have to bury comrades as in Indochina, kill the innocent and leave, abandon everything amidst hate and contempt? Were all these patient efforts to make France respected in peace going to be compromised? Was this an exercise in futility? Larcher's eyes brimmed as he looked at his two officers. They were young. They belonged to a generation pledged to liquidating a past full of prestige. Given his age, he had known the victory over the Germans, the liberation of Paris, the Alsace campaign. But this joy had been very short lived. He had found himself in Indochina to wage a harsh and inhuman war. He felt suddenly overcome by an immense weariness.

"My friends, we have done what we could. We have done our duty. From now on, the whole business is beyond our control. The year 1956 will be difficult. It is the wind of history. Let us try to be equal to our task."

CHAPTER XVII

Reality sometimes caught up with dreams, thought Salah, standing in the courtyard of the *mechouar*, the Sultan's palace. The night before, he had left Goulimine in a Mercedes placed at his disposal by the Governor and, with Moulay Mehdi, his son Mahmoud, and Hassan ould Bouali, his counselor, had driven through the magnificent Moroccan countryside. His mind was a blank. He was not his usual self, but agitated by what he saw—the well-kept fields covered by crowds of peasants irrigating the land and weeding and pruning trees, asphalt roads, impressive buildings, the cities he traveled through. But what struck the old nomad chief even more strongly was the density of the population, the swarms of people in the fields, in towns, in the public squares, on the roads, in vehicles.

Here, within the *mechouar*, the measures taken for the

sovereign's welcoming ceremony on the occasion of the celebration of the Feast of the Sacrifice surpassed anything a
nomad could imagine. The tribal chiefs and their delegations
had been arranged in several rows along three sides of the
immense courtyard. They had their backs to the lawn's flow-
erbeds located in front of the Morrish-Spanish-style building
with round glazed tiles and the arches of the doorways adorned
with quotations from the Koran. Geometric motifs inter-
twined in masterly patterns covered the building's entire
facade and the main entrance. Facing the crowd of dignitaries
on the other side of the road, from which the sovereign's arrival
was expected, closing off the fourth side of the rectangular
courtyard, a host of horsemen from the mountain tribes of the
central and southern part of Morocco had come to pay tribute
to His Majesty. Salah was fascinated by this sight.

The horses, lined up in four rows, were fitted out with Arab
saddles with their typical pommels, high cantles, and large
stirrups. All of the visible part of saddle leather was studded
with copper nails gleaming in the sun. The horses—most of
them of medium size, mixed Arabian thoroughbreds with long
manes—pawed the ground impatiently and neighed. Some
tried to rear up, but were chastened by horsemen who pulled
savagely at the double bit of the harnesses and brought them
back into line. With their large straw hats falling over their
shoulders, their felt caps on their heads, their multicolored
burnooses, their soft leather boots of red *Filali*, the horsemen
were a noble sight. In their right hands they held their rifles,
with the large and flat butt ends and outsized barrels, which
they would use that evening for the *fantasia*, that frenzied
charge which they would ride that evening in honor of the
Sultan. Rising in their stirrups, in a whirl of dust and cries, they
would as a man discharge their weapons. Salah was impressed
by the physiques of these warriors, their faces furrowed with
wrinkles and deeply marked by the rough weather, their tense
bodies, their feverish eyes sunken in their sockets, wild gleams

lurking in their gazes. The skulls under the caps were shaved, but the rings of beard which highlighted the bony profiles of the faces made them resemble those predatory birds which are always starving and never sated. They called to each other in an unfamiliar language with raucous and guttural sounds. Behind the compact, moving mass of horsemen one could sense more than see the enormous, gawking crowd which rippled like the sea, come to witness the arrival of the Moroccan Sultan, held back by lines of affable police.

Suddenly a vague and rapidly swelling murmur was heard. Thousands of voices repeated in unison, *Yahya El Malik*, "Long live the king." The words filled the void and stopped once the procession had reached the courtyard. Silence reigned at the moment the king emerged from his limousine. He made his appearance preceded by dignitaries and the master of ceremonies. A frail figure in a *jellaba*, a simple robe of pure white linen that fell in straight folds, he wore a strange headdress of gray felt, nipped at the peak by a lengthwise stripe. He advanced in front of the horsemen, raising his arm in a salute, a half-smile fixed on his face. Then he turned toward the tribal chieftains, whom he saluted one by one as they were presented by the chief of protocol. The emotions of the dignitaries were intense. Some fell to their knees while others tried to prostrate themselves in accordance with the Oriental tradition, but the king, giving them a tap on the shoulder, suggested in a gentle tone that they rise. Others tried to kiss his hand, which he energetically withdrew, still keeping his smile. Yet others, taking advantage of the bodyguards' lack of vigilance, literally fell into his arms. When the king reached Salah the latter bent over, trying to embrace his right shoulder, but in the shuffle his head landed on the king's sleeve, to which he fervently pressed his mouth. Stuttering and stammering, he uttered unintelligible words, but he heard the master of ceremonies call out his name and status. At the word Reguibat the king paused and inquired after the health of Salah ould Ahmed and his companions—who, struck dumb with emotion, their eyes reflecting the greatest embarrassment, understood barely half of what the monarch was saying.

After these presentations, the tribal chieftains and their delegations were invited to enter the huge, long reception hall of the *mechouar*, with its floor covered with *chichaoua* rugs of curly wool. At the end of the hall, on a tapestry-hung dais, the king was seated in an armchair. Once the room was full, he rose, went toward the microphone set in front of him, and read his speech in a monotone. Salah rejoiced at having brought along in his entourage his counselor Hassan ould Bouali, a scholar of classical Arabic, who in a low voice translated the Sultan's words to the delegation in the Hassaniya dialect, the only language understandable to the Reguibat. To be sure, Salah and his companions knew the Koran by heart. But the language used by the Moroccan sovereign differed both in accent and in sentence structure from the religious language, and they had difficulty in following the speaker's thoughts. Hassan translated the following speech to the delegation:

"Faithful subjects of the Sahara, one of the most ardent wishes which we have been cherishing for a long time was to receive you here. I am vastly overjoyed to be here with you, to be able to talk with men renowned for their knowledge of religion and of law, and to hear you reaffirm, as did your ancestors, your fiedlity to the Alaouit throne, and your attachment to the Moroccan nation, one and indivisible. Your coming here coincides with an ancient and beautiful tradition established by the Moroccan sovereigns who periodically embarked on study and reconnaissance trips through your Sahara to reaffirm the unity of the country and to inform themselves regarding the needs of the population. My grandfather, Moulay Hassan—may Allah rest his soul—made two visits to the Sahara to consolidate the unity of Morocco and his sovereignty over all of the national territory at a time when it was jealously eyed by foreigners. Today, Allah be praised, circumstances allow me to renew tradition and to receive the Saharan tribal chieftains who have come to pay homage to their sovereign. You are welcome. I have given orders to my ministers and administration to take advantage of your presence and study existing problems with each of you, and to lend an attentive ear to your grievances. We have decided to continue to work to improve your living conditions and to ensure that you make progress in the religious, social, economic, and cultural spheres. We have also determined to see to it that your regions share in the benefits of independence, freedom, and newfound dignity, and that you realize your hopes, which are ours as well, and those of all your Moroccan compatriots. I pay tribute to all the sacrifices you have made to remain Moroccan in the face of everyone and everything. I solemnly pledge to continue my course of action through all possible diplomatic and military means to return our Sahara to the motherland, with due respect for its historic rights and the will of its inhabitants. Thus I will feel I have carried out the mission entrusted to me by Allah, restoring the past and building a future of happiness and serenity for all my subjects, in the north as well as in the south of the country."

After the speech (which was listened to in religious silence and warmly applauded) when their names were called out, the tribal chieftains were invited to give a brief response to the Sultan. When his turn came Salah, who had gotten up his courage, took care to avoid politics in his remarks. He explained that, as a descendant of Sid Ahmed Reguibi, he, like his ancestors, had always respected the spiritual authority of the "Emir of the faithful." Thus today he was proud to have been able to attend His Majesty and through him to bear witness to the high consideration in which the Reguibat held Morocco, a brotherly and sovereign country.

In doing this, and by speaking on a purely religious level, Salah had avoided the forbidden words of allegiance and independence. Instinctively he had felt that, all things considered and due allowance being made, he was in a way a head of state who respected his neighbor but who wished to preserve his autonomy. Likewise, he had avoided agreeing with all his colleagues who had preceded him, and who had made extensive, offensive remarks directed at the negative effects of the colonial period. To Moulay Mehdi, who immediately reproached him for not having further committed himself, Salah answered that one had to bear in mind the specific nature of the Reguibat, who had received independence solely from Allah.

Surprised by the somewhat archaic style of expression used by Salah in his reply and by his unusual vocabulary, the king turned several times to his counselors for clarification of the precise meaning of certain words. He thanked Salah with a deep bow of the head and let his gaze rest for a moment on the delegation of these men in blue with whom he was not well acquainted, these men who were so different from the "Tekna" or "Ait oussa" tribes.

After the exchange of speeches the king rose, thanked his guests in a short sentence, and disappeared through a door into the palace, followed by the entire court. A horde of black servants in red *chéchias* and white tunics brought in round tables and tea-trays, and placed dishes of food before each delegation with startling speed. The meal was abundant, and varied. The *tajins*, the clay pots with simmering stews, succeeded each other. Then there were different kinds of *couscous*, with raisins, cinnamon, and spices, and oven-roasted sheep. Salah and his companions, distrustful of the rich and spicy dishes of Moroccan cuisine, tasted everything circumspectly. In the general hubbub the Reguibat delegation was quiet, admiring in silence—while exchanging knowing looks— the agility and efficiency of the servers, the richness of the dishes, the softness of the curly wool carpets woven in the upper Atlas Mountains. They admired everything, amazed.

After the meal, Salah and his companions returned to the room given them in the gardens surrounding the palace of their hosts. The pavilion stood in the center of a bright green arbor. Water flowed clear and limpid along the drains, here and there splashing abruptly onto the surrounding lawns. The next day the delegation was invited to the Friday one o'clock prayers, which were to be led by the Sultan himself. Salah, standing not far from the king, who officiated as the Imam, alone before the crowd of the faithful, was in a highly emotional state. He had finally achieved his dream and was reciting the ritual prayer behind the Prince of Believers. Now he could die serene. He would have liked to express his joy and gratitude to the sovereign, but as soon as the prayer ended the king quickly crossed through the ranks of the faithful. Having reached the courtyard of a mosque, he mounted a magnificent white horse led by one of his black servants, while another, in accordance with tradition, walked at his side, holding an enormous square parasol over his head to protect him from the sun's rays. Though he always admired ceremonial state displays, Salah nevertheless found this custom of the parasol odd. As a true nomad he somewhat regretted this pomp and protocol. He would have liked to see the Sultan stroll among the faithful and chat with them.

On their return from the Great Prayer Salah's companions began packing their things for the next day's trip back to Goulimine, still in the Governor's Mercedes. They slipped off to the *souk* to make their last purchases, for they wished to buy small trifles, shawls, caskets, and jewels, which they would then try to send on to their families through the south of Morocco, using the good offices of seasoned caravaneers. Tired from the ceremonies, Salah preferred to remain alone, sitting on the grass in front of the guest room and contemplating the beautiful layout of the gardens spread out before him. The scent of coniferous and flowering trees filled the air, as well as the characteristic odor of *tuyas* from which the Moroccans made chests inlaid with mother-of-pearl which, when opened, gave off the scent of Moroccan forests.

For the rest of his life he would never forget the two days he had just spent. He could not help thinking with a shiver of the speed of events. Everything had gone very fast. Moulay Mehdi had arrived at his encampment with great ceremony, and in his abrupt manner, to which it was difficult to reply, had explained to him the urgent need to pay a visit to the Sultan. With his usual ardor he had swept away Salah's reservations, and they had left for Goulimin, which they reached in five days. They stayed in the huge but dirty house of a well-to-do tradesman located in the midst of a market. And on the occasion of the great sacrifice they had been invited by the king.

He had a bad conscience about Larcher. To be sure, he had made very clear to him his wish to go and pay homage to the king, but nevertheless he did not want to burn his bridges with the French administration, with which he had just managed to renew good relations in such a spectacular manner. Thus, before his departure for Goulimin, he had penned a long letter to the commander in which he explained the reasons of a religious nature which led him to make this trip. He had assured Larcher in warm and friendly terms of his loyalty both to him personally and to the administration he so worthily represented. He had also stated that during his absence he had delegated the duties incumbent on him to his older son, and asked Larcher to consider this choice as indicative of his desire to maintain close ties with France. His elder son, young, dedicated, and competent, whose courage and spirit of initiative had been tried and tested in the Mahmoud affair, had a certain influence on the Sidi Allal. In Salah's absence he could be counted on for sensitive guidance of this turbulent tribe.

He had written that, but at heart he was secretly afraid that Larcher's predictions would in fact come true. He recalled in detail the interesting discussion in the encampment when he had brought Mahmoud back to him. The commander's arguments had some validity. He recognized that now. The ambiguity persisted. The king had in fact thanked them for their act

of allegiance. His visit therefore had had the political over-
tones that Larcher had predicted. To be sure, he had replied
prudently to the king's speech, keeping solely to the religious
aspect, but the Moroccan press, which had been read to him
that very morning, did not stress that. It stated that he had
come to make an act of submission to the Sultan. He had
certainly not appreciated that interpretation, but what could
be done? He had been overtaken. Likewise, he did not appreciate the reactions of his companions. They were all ready to go
farther than he, to fall into line under the Moroccan flag, to
declare themselves Moroccan subjects. Moulay Mehdi, whose
sympathies for Morocco were still keen, was beginning to
irritate him because of the fanaticism he displayed. Moreover,
that Liberation Army was causing him some concern. He had
not yet had the opportunity to talk with the Moroccan authorities about that, to show his opposition to that organization,
but he already knew that young nomads had enlisted in it.
When he expressed in private his anger at this recruitment, he
had found Mahmoud, his beloved son, apparently receptive to
Moroccan propaganda. He still had to be on the alert, and here
too Larcher seemed to have been right.

CHAPTER XVIII

The four vehicles of the light patrol headed by de La Renaudie crawled along the cliff, stopping from time to time to allow the trackers to pick up possible trails. Nothing interesting had come to light during the bleak three-day trip in which de La Renaudie and Vogel had been entrusted with a mounted platoon to keep a watch on the northern frontier at the end of the Spanish zone. It was almost four o'clock in the afternoon, and they decided to bivouac on the Hamada, a spreading, arid terrain which was immensely flat. Vogel was suffering from idleness since, from the start of the trip, he had not encountered a single tent, as was often the case in these sensitive zones; he and his guide had seen the fresh tracks of a wild, large-horned sheep, however. While the platoon was setting up he decided briefly to skirt the cliff to see whether by chance he might get a shot at the animal. Amused, de La Renaudie recommended that he not go too far and return to the encampment before sunset.

Vogel took a Mas-36 gun—which he preferred to any other automatic or semi-automatic weapon because it never jammed—and a few bullets, and set off in search of the wild sheep tracks. He reached them easily after walking a few hundred meters. The animal had come to the Hamada less than an hour ago to feast on fresh grass in the hollows of the sandy depressions, and then had gone back down to the gorge. The terrain at this point of the cliff was fascinatingly beautiful. The subsidiary mountain chain of the Ouarkziz died out south of the Oued Drâa in a tangle of cliffs, peaks, crags, landslides, and rocks. This geological chaos contrasted with the bleak gray plateau of Hamada, a riot of color—yellow, violet, black, blue, red, along with mineral substances including sandstone, limestone, basalt, granite, and clay. In addition, the fading day, clear and fresh but with the sun still hot, created an atmosphere of great limpidity, and the echo of each stone which slid out from under the steps of the man walking and fell into the precipice echoed into infinity with unusual resonance.

Vogel tore himself away from his thoughts. Only two hours of daylight remained. He had to move fast to intercept the wild sheep. He took a small path which followed the contours of the cliff halfway down the slope and overlooked the gorge below. After having gone a hundred meters he caught sight of the wild sheep below, a magnificent male with large horns twisting backwards, grazing on a rock balanced over the precipice. Vogel took aim at the shoulder joint, but just at the moment he was about to fire, the animal made an extraordinary jump and landed five meters lower on another rock. Vogel swore, but appreciated the beauty of the leap into the void and the sureness of the animal's step. He aimed again but the beast, now on guard since it must have seen him, continued to jump from rock to rock with amazing grace and precision. It landed on flat land in the valley. There was no possibility of following it along the same path. Vogel advanced twenty meters, giving him a broader view of the gorge. As he had expected, he saw the animal trotting off toward the west. The distance was considerable, but he decided to try his luck. He crouched down, set the sight at 200, aimed calmly, and fired. The bullet hit the sheep's hindquarters and the animal slowed down, sagging onto its hind legs. But it continued to advance, limping and quickly disappeared into the barren rocks. Vogel understood that the game was up. One and a half hours of daylight remained; he would have had to go back to the encampment, take two men with him, go down into the gorge, kill the animal, and bring it back up. The operation required too much time. Vogel discharged the gun, forced the empty cartridge case out of the breech and out of habit loaded a bullet into the gun.

He turned around. It was then that he saw, on the same road which he needed to take to find his way back, a man, gun in hand, who had stopped at the bend in the road and was scrutinizing him. Vogel's blood froze. The man's clothing told him that he was a rebel. Wearing a dirty Balaclava helmet, the man carried two hand-grenades in the pockets of his kaki battle shirt. He wore the flowing pants of the Reguibat *meharistes*, but on his feet were brown-laced boots. He was alone. Vogel's thoughts raced at top speed. He was glad he had put a bullet in the gun, but if he raised the weapon to his shoulder, even quickly, the man might do likewise—and might be faster on the draw. It was going to be a close duel, and the outcome was certain one of them would die, or maybe both. There was no possibility for maneuvering or for diversionary tactics on this narrow path overhanging the precipice. Vogel suddenly thought that, given the short distance, he could fire from the hip. But the rebel did not move, and he hesitated to fire first. In any case, surprise tactics wouldn't work, since the man undoubtedly had the same ideas he did. All these thoughts lasted for only a few seconds. Still undecided, Vogel decided to speak.

"Hello."

"Hello."

"Can we talk?"

"Yes, sure. I suppose you're Vogel, the officer-interpreter from Tindouf."

"That's right. And you're Lahcen ould Labid of the Sidi Mahmoud batallion."

"That's me," answered Lahcen smiling. "I think we can sit down." The two men sat down cross-legged, their guns lying on their knees. The tension was lessening. Each now knew with whom he was dealing.

"Are your men far from here?" asked Vogel.

"No, not very far. Behind that gorge I was chasing the wild sheep and ran across the tracks of the same animal you just wounded. A nice shot. Are you going to go get the animal?"

"No, it's too far off. I'll leave it for you. Your men can have a feast. Are there many of you?"

"No, I have thirty with me. All Reguibat."

At this point Vogel felt it was worth trying for a serious talk. What did he risk now? Lahcen obviously did not intend to get into a Wild-West gun duel. At best, they would part as good friends while sticking to their different political positions.

"Listen," began Vogel, "I'm going to talk to you man to man. This is January 1958. Two years ago, in 1956, the Reguibat started enlisting in the Moroccan Liberation Army. That MLA was supposed to liberate the Sahara from foreign— Spanish and French—presence. What's the situation today? You've been harassing our posts without any tangible results: Oum El Achar, where we lost two men, including the lieutenant who was assassinated by his men; Tinfouchy, where a captain and his driver, alone in a jeep, were killed; Merkala, where another captain was killed, as well as fourteen or fifteen of your men. On the Spanish side you've hardly achieved any better results, and you were cut off from your encampment, from your families, from your friends. I don't want to discuss the motive that brought you to Morocco. I understand it. The Sultan had just come back to his throne and Morocco became independent. You're offered arms, responsibilities, a good salary, and a goal to achieve. Over two years, however, you should have understood that you've been used, manipulated, and that you've been doing other people's work. As far as I know this land is not Moroccan and never has been."

"Since you're speaking to me frankly, I'll do the same," Lahcen answered Vogel. "What you're saying is true. Two years ago we enlisted enthusiastically in the Moroccan Liberation Army. Our old chiefs—I'm thinking especially of Salah ould Ahmed, the chief of the confederation—set an example by pledging allegiance to the Sultan immediately upon his return. The Moroccans dazzled us with the ideas of the departure of the French and the Spanish from the Sahara. But two years later we see that in reality we've been taken in. The Moroccans used us to get back the Sahara, but for their own ends. They believe that it's their land. But it's the land of the Reguibat. So too we learn that negotiations are under way between the Spanish and the Moroccan governments regarding the occupied territories in the south of the Oued Drâa. Spain, we are told, intends to yield part of that territory and its posts of Tizgui-Rempt and Tantan to the Moroccans. The Treaties of the Protectorates, signed in 1911 between Spain and Morocco, did not take into account the desires of the inhabitants of that country. Those treaties are now outdated. But one thing is certain: it is that the inhabitants of those territories are still there. The Spanish and French governments should not ignore the fact that this land has never belonged to the Moroccans and that has been so since time immemorial. It's the land on which Allah treated us and had us live in peace and inviolability. If Spain since 1911 has not consulted us it's because at the time we were not up-to-date on world politics. But times have changed, and we've learned a lot of things since the independence of Morocco."

"In those conditions," interrupted Vogel, "why not give up MLA, in which you're treated with suspicion, and go over in Tindouf?"

Had the suggestion been too direct, too brutal? Vogel was a bit sorry he had said that. An amused smile was on Lahcen's face, but he did not answer.

"Got a cigarette?"

"No, I don't smoke. And I didn't think I'd run into you today." They both laughed. From the small leather pouch he wore around his neck, Lahcen took out his smoking gear: a small, hollow, dried sheep bone, which he carefully filled with tobacco and lit up. Having inhaled two or three puffs of this dried grass mixture, he continued the conversation.

"No question but that we're suspect. You're right, we are. The Moroccans sometimes irritate our sensibilities through ignorance of our customs, our language, and our religion. And then, you know the nomads. They're starting to get tired of the Moroccans."

"Sure," answered Vogel. "The fickleness of the Reguibat is well known, and if I were the Moroccans I would do what they do—I would distrust you."

They both laughed again.

"The idea of going over to France with all of my men," continued Lahcen, "is one I've had several times. But the operation seems difficult to me in more ways than one. Some of my men have their families in the Oued Drâa. Our comings and goings are closely monitored by the Royal Army. Finally, we don't know what conditions would be imposed by France for our going over. Would you have any ideas about that?"

Vogel sensed the man's agitation. It was time to seize the opportunity without reflecting too long. Head lowered, he launched into a series of conditions which seemed to him in keeping with the Command's philosophy.

"The surrender of military deserters goes beyond my competence for the time being. I think it could be accepted except for those who have committed murder. As for the surrender of the nomads who took up arms against us, it could be compatible with a request for *Aman*. In other words, seeking an official pardon. Therefore, it would be unconditional. Pardon would be granted as long as they hand over their arms to the authorities."

"Once they've gone over, are you planning to make use of the men in my company?"

"I don't know what the attitude of my authorities is about that. Personally, I think they should be used in their areas of specialization, as guides, informants, advance frontier sentinels. They could be formed into an auxiliary unit of our troops under the same command. Why not?"

"Your program is tempting. If it were accepted by your authorities could you let me know?"

The two men then decided to reach agreement on a capitulation plan. Together they unloaded their weapons and shook hands. Sitting down next to each other they quickly found a common language. Lahcen had fine features, two feverish black eyes, and a small beard on his chin. Vogel was struck by his intelligence, his caustic wit, and his organizational sense. It was agreed that he would send one of his men to Tindouf. To avoid alerting the Moroccans through an indiscretion, he would go not to Vogel's office but to the *caid* of Tajakant, Mantallah ould Senhouri. Vogel would go also to the *caid*, who would be notified in advance. He would give the emissary a letter for Lahcen explaining France's conditions for a surrender and the procedures for retrieving Lahcen's group with arms and baggage, using trucks to bring back the families of the men who had surrendered. The men would be brought here in a week, and in the meantime Lahcen would undertake to bring the men's families closer to the frontier to facilitate the recovery operation.

The last rays of sunlight lit up the horizon. It was time to end this intense conversation which was taking place in most extraordinary conditions. They agreed to keep the whole matter very quiet in order not to jeopardize the process they had started and to avoid causing the Reguibat serious difficulties. As they parted Lahcen took Vogel's arm and said spontaneously, "I'll give you a token of my good will and the purity of my intentions. Take my gun. It's yours."

It was a Mas-49 of French origin, more sophisticated than the Mas-36, for it was a semi-automatic, doubtless retrieved from a deserter. Through the registration number, thought Vogel, it could be traced and its former owner identified. The two men shook hands emotionally and set off in opposite directions. Back at the encampment Vogel hid the gun among some rocks where it would be easy to find. To avoid suspicion, he did not want to come back to his men with two guns. De La Renaudie greeted his aide coolly, reproaching him for having returned very late. Vogel explained his meeting.

"All that's very interesting," agreed de La Renaudie, "but Lahcen now knows that we're here." That was sheer common sense. The most elementary form of prudence indeed was dictated, given the presence of thirty well-armed rebels hundreds of meters away. The two officers decided to reinforce the sentinels with extra men placed on strategic points along the rocks to watch over the exits onto the cliff. All the men were placed on alert, and assigned to keep watch in turn. Radio broadcasts were started up again. The orders were strict. The advance sentinels hidden in the hollows of the boulders were instructed to fire without warning on anyone moving toward Hamada from the frontier.

A tense atmosphere reigned in the camp. Following the measures taken by de La Renaudie, all the men were prepared for a rough night. The stars gleamed in a crystal-clear and cloudless sky. The air was dry and bitingly cold. Vogel took de La Renaudie aside to retrieve Lahcen's gun, which he had left a dozen meters from the camp. They wrapped the weapon in an old rag and slipped it under the front seat of the commander's car without their men knowing.

The two officers hardly slept at all that night. They checked several times to see that the sentries had not dozed off and went on several inspection rounds. Vogel seemed quite calm. He was convinced that Lahcen had not set a trap for him and that everything would take place as they had agreed. De La Renaudie, who was well aware of the importance of the matter, was more skeptical.

"To sum it up," he asked Vogel, "what do you think of this interesting turn of events?"

"In considering coming over, the Reguibat are guided by several considerations. First of all, they've got a definite liking for change—if possible, in their own interests. The fickleness of the nomads is well known. They've also been disappointed by the Moroccan promises, by the clumsiness of the Moroccan administration, by the various irritants which occur between two ethnic groups who don't always understand each other. Spain also seems to have disappointed them for reasons which I don't quite grasp, but primarily because Madrid is negotiating with Morocco to abandon these territories. But what strikes me about the young, more progressive Reguibat who've received part of their education in Morocco is the emergence of nationalism—a diffuse nationalism but a real one. The upcoming independence of Mauritania is making them think. Who knows whether they're not considering the seeds of a Saharan and nomadic state? That feeling of belonging to a different ethnic group—on a land which is theirs—makes one envisage, sooner or later, difficulties for Morocco. If, as seems probable, Morocco persists in its policy of the annexation of the territory abandoned by Spain, it is likely to be faced with nomads who have studied at Moroccan or Spanish universities."

"But in rallying to Tindouf," commented de La Renaudie, "they're coming to Algeria. Are they aware of that?"

"Not exactly. For them Tindouf means first of all France. But if independence were achieved tomorrow, and the Algerians succeeded us, there's a strong chance that our Reguibat allies would once again head off toward Morocco, saying that they had erred."

The night was very calm. At dawn the last sentries were relieved. The men, who had suffered from the cold all night, lit huge fires to warm themselves and prepared the morning tea. Lahcen had not tried to attack the French camp. De La Renaudie went up to Vogel and, not saying a word, the two men shook hands with a knowing smile.

Clearly the process of surrender had begun.

CHAPTER XIX

The first *arganiers*, small robust trees with glossy leaves which grow on the rocky slopes of the Atlas Mountain chain, appeared along the side of the winding road. The presence of those trees, known for the pungent oil of their berries, marked the border between the fertile plains of the north and the barren lands of the Moroccan south. They marked the end of the intensive cultivation of grain fields, wheat, barley, oats, rye, fruits, and vegetables. They marked the beginning of the harsh and severe landscape of the mountains, pastures for goats, sparse crops around scattered water sources. The *arganiers* also marked the transition from oaks, hazel trees, eucalyp-

199

tus trees, and date-palms. The latter extended from Taroudant to Goulimin in a riot of all shades of green, in isolated thickets at the bottom of steep gorges or lands with ochre soil, in thick and shaggy oases with palm trees waving in the wind.

Tired from the linear monotony of the plain, the Mercedes' driver accelerated suddenly, hitting the first turns with renewed zeal. He doubtless unconsciously wanted a change of rhythm and took the turns at a spirited clip. Salah, who had been dozing with his *cheche* covering his head and face down to his mouth, grasped the door handle and shot him an angry look. In a tone that brooked no retort, he told the driver to slow down. He did not like these car trips. He always sat in front despite the demands of protocol since he thought he could thus better manage the nausea which overcame him on each trip.

Salah was returning from Rabat, Morocco in a sullen mood. He had been summoned there by the Minister of the Interior, who once again had reproached him for his intransigent attitude toward the Moroccan Liberation Army and the weakness of his commitment to the king's ideas. Once again Salah had expounded his theories on these two topics, and had pointed out to him that his allegiance to His Majesty, whom he admired, was solely of a religious and not of a political nature. The Moroccans pretended not to understand the subtlety of his reasoning, and the result was a dialogue of the deaf. In a nutshell, he had once again been preached to by an administration exasperated by his behavior. He was tired. In a few hours he would again be in Goulimine. He was beginning to know this road by heart. He had taken this road with a joyful heart and light spirit nearly five years before to meet the king for the first time. He recalled that first visit to Rabat, so enthusiastic and euphoric. Then he had marveled at everything in this country, which he was discovering now that he was over sixty: the beauty of the landscapes, the kindness of the population, the friendly attitude of the authorities, and above all the Prince of Believers—sensitive and frail in his cotton *jellaba* like a diaphanous porcelain object, his enigmatic smile, his lordly mien, and his gentle voice.

The enchantment did not last. A guest of the Moroccan government, with all of the Reguibat dignitaries who had followed him, Salah was put under the administrative command of the governor of Goulimin. He immediately understood that it would be difficult for him to return home soon. The border with Algeria was closed. He was being sought by the French authorities, ready to throw him in prison if he appeared on the Reguibat lands. Or that at least was the claim of the Moroccans who did all they could to keep him under their supervision. Salah quickly realized that the friendliness of the local authorities, who had a great deal of money at their disposal to seduce the nomad population, had no lack of ulterior motives. He disliked the governor, an obsequious and paunchy man always dressed in a three-piece suit. The lower part of his face had friendly wrinkles, while his gaze remained cold. This Governor, doubtless obeying orders from his superiors, had tried from the outset to use the prestige of Salah's name to conduct a recruitment campaign for the Liberation Army among the Reguibat nomads. Salah, loyal to his principles, had most vehemently opposed this. He repeated what he had already said in the past to Larcher: if Morocco thought that the territory south of Drâa belonged to it, which was disputed by many, it could enter into negotiations with the occupying powers, Spain and France, as it had done to achieve its own independence. The Liberation Army, therefore, was good for nothing, Salah had reaffirmed to the governor. If, however, the Moroccan authorities, for whatever reasons of their own, believed that they should wage a struggle, they were welcome to recruit Moroccan subjects of His Majesty. But why wish to enlist young Reguibat and have them die for an ideal that was not even theirs?

His position, unfortunately, could not hold out in that atmosphere and in the face of pressure from the Moroccan authorities. After having hesitated for a while in the face of such determination, the Governor quickly realized that he had to isolate Salah, who, deprived of the support of his tribe, would no longer have the power to exert influence or impose his will. While feigning to give consideration to the arguments of the Reguibat chief, the representative of the Moroccan administration, through a careful campaign of persuasion, convinced the other Reguibat chiefs of Salah's entourage. It was thus that Salah learned one day that his own counselor, Hassan ould Bouali, had agreed to serve the kingdom with the blessing of Moulay Medhi, and was entrusted with the command of a company of one hundred men, to be chosen from among the Reguibat of Legouacem. Salah was enraged. He had harsh words for his friends and for Hassan, of whom he was very fond. But the surprises were not over; a few days later his son Mahmoud, who was always by his side, announced to him that he had decided to join the Moroccan Liberation Army. The meeting was a stormy one. Salah had begun by being stern and curt, trying to play on his paternal authority. His son, who seemed dead set, had not flinched and had stuck to his intention. Salah, now the grieved father, had tried persuasion through gentleness and feeling. He had recalled the memory of his mother, and the promises he had made to her when she died that he would care for Mahmoud. He spoke to him of the efforts he had made to free him from French prisons, the risks he might run, but in the end Mahmoud had left without a word, brushing his lips to him in a kiss. For several months Salah had been totally depressed.

Bad luck seemed to have mounted a campaign against him. The news that reached him from Algeria had not been good. In March 1957 General de Gaulle, whom he so greatly admired, had come to Tindouf and had met all the Reguibat and Tajakant chiefs. He had given them assurances regarding the solicitude France would continue to show toward the Reguibat regardless of political developments. He had been unable to go

General de Gaulle visits Tindouf

to Tindouf at that time and was furious at not having shaken the hand of that great man, that great Frenchman. In June 1958 Vogel had under his command Lahcen ould Labid and his thirty men. That news, which caused commotion and consternation among the Moroccans, had rather amused him, and he secretly paid homage to Lahcen for having made the courageous decision to go over to France. A month later, in February 1958, a joint French-Spanish operation in the Tiriz, the Zemour, and the Spanish Sahara had enabled Vogel through Lahcen ould Labid, to make peace with the company of Hassan ould Bouali with a total of 117 men with arms and baggage. It was with hope that he saw those men go over, for he thought that his son Mahmoud might be among them, having abandoned the struggle. But he was bitterly disappointed when he learned that Mahmoud had refused to yield, had retreated following the military operation into the former Spanish Morocco and was continuing the fight.

Decidedly, his family was a cause of great concern to him. He had learned that his son Ahmed, to whom he had entrusted command of the tribe, had gotten married during the spring of 1959 to a woman of the Foqra tribe from Ahel Lemjed. He had been very irritated, for he considered the marriage a misalliance. He had written a very stern letter to his son, asking him to end the marriage and to get back on the right path. But Ahmed, very much in love with the beautiful Foqra woman and made much of by his in-laws, had not even bothered to answer him. Salah, who could not conceive of marriage aside from the Brahim ou Daoud, was badly mortified by this attitude. A few months later, he learned that his son Mahmoud, who was fighting in the Ouarkziz, had become engaged to a Sellam woman. He exploded in a furious rage. He dictated a very violent letter to his son in which he reminded him that not only was he about to marry the daughter of a tribe that was a dependent of the Sidi Allal, but he had also been forced to kill a Sellam in self-defense. To his great surprise he received an affectionate reply from Mahmoud. The latter explained that he loved the young girl and that ideas of vassaldom and dependency were gone, had disappeared following the independence of Morocco. All the tribes were now on an equal footing, and he believed that it was not a misalliance to become engaged to this Sellam. Salah ould Ahmed understood nothing of this political democratic language. He shrugged his shoulders and spoke of it no more.

At the entrance to Goulimin the Mercedes was stopped by an administration car. An official, formal as ever, who had been expecting Salah's arrival, requested him to go at once to the house of Moulay Mehdi, in the marketplace, where an important meeting of the Reguibat was expecting him. Salah, who would have liked to go back to the tent which he had set up two kilometers from Goulimine in the midst of the countryside to get away from the walls of the houses, was vexed but, given the official's insistence, agreed to accept this odd invitation.

Salah did not like Moulay Mehdi's house, which the latter had bought from a tradesman in town. It was large, to be sure, but dark, badly kept, and dirty. When he entered the large reception room he found a big group assembled, sitting on mats along the walls and waiting for him. Everyone rose when he entered. He greeted each of them, happy to once again see old companions, and flattered to receive homage from new and as yet unfamiliar faces. Moulay Mehdi embraced him effusively, more intensely than usual. Salah was amused and touched by this sign of affection and long-standing camaraderie. He sat down, as did the whole company after him, and requested that tea be served, behaving a bit as though he were at home.

Moulay Mehdi then took the floor with no further delay. This was a time for sadness, he explained. The Reguibat, a valorous people, had just suffered a setback in battle. The news was bad, and because of his age he had neither the courage nor the strength to announce it. He preferred to leave that task to Lemkisser, a young Reguibi, the only witness to the battle that had taken place.

Contrary to all expectations, Salah wanted to intervene right away in the sententious manner he usually used in extraordinary circumstances. He thanked Moulay Mehdi but scolded him gently for the despair which he displayed. The Reguibat, he continued, were a great people which, from 1890 until 1934, the date of the arrival of the French, had given battle to their enemies more than a hundred times to affirm their supremacy over the twenty tribes which shared the western Sahara. In 1907, after a three-day battle at Foucht, they had crushed their last opponents, the Oulad Bousbaaa. If, therefore, they had suffered a setback today, that was no catastrophe. He reminded Moulay Mehdi that he had to pull himself together. He belonged to the tribe of Brahim ou Daoud, whose symbol was the spiritual camel, "which can be caught by caressing it, but which tramples men underfoot if frightened."

The crowd did not react to these words, words which usually evoked exclamations of feigned admiration. The generally good-natured public liked to hear these platitudes, interpreted as the manifestation of the wisdom of the great, insofar as they were set forward in a peremptory manner by a recognized authority. But Salah realized that the atmosphere was heavy and that minds were elsewhere. He therefore invited Lemkisser to tell him what had happened.

Habib oul M'Ribet and twenty of his men had tried to set up an ambush on the Tantan road to waylay the Spanish army convoys. The idea as such was not a bad one, and the site for the ambush seemed well chosen. It was a bend in the pebbly road dominated by two small hillocks. Habib, who was a courageous man but relatively inexperienced in such matters, had set up his small troops badly, twenty Reguibat armed with repeating rifles and a Bren-gun. He had placed his men in a semicircle, but had not thought to keep an echelon in the rear capable of covering any retreat of the attackers in case of a response from the Spanish side. What was more, while the set-up of the troops seemed appropriate, the terrain behind Habib's group was too flat and bare. Another detail turned out to be of the greatest importance for the Reguibat; a deep ditch ran along the edge of the road.

At first the ambush seemed to be set in the best possible conditions. Two open troop transports, not very far apart, with soldiers sitting facing each other, their backs to the road, changed speed to go up the hill and thus slowed down. Habib discharged the first burst of gunfire from his automatic Bren-gun, which killed the driver of the first vehicle on the spot. But the officer, unhurt, jumped to the ground on the other side of the road, and with great presence of mind started giving orders in a clear and apparently unemotional voice. Bounding off their trucks, the Spaniards were mowed down by bullets which they encountered head-on, and collapsed over the rails without a sound, like marionettes. The second vehicle, slightly behind the first, which was subjected to lighter fire, immediately pulled up to the rescue. The survivors, displaying the reflexes of hunted animals, slid into the ditch, thus disappearing from the sight of Ibrahim and his men. Protected by the height of the ditch, they began calmly firing, shooting from a reclining position with formidable precision.

Then, disregarding the orders given, Mahmoud, joyfully intoxicated at having killed two Spaniards, charged, hair flying in the wind, in an assault on the trucks. He shouted, "Allahu ak . . . Allah is the gr . . ." He was not able to finish the sentence. Then and there he crumpled backwards, a bullet between his eyes. Four of his comrades who tried doing the same thing were cut down the same way. Faced with the loss of five of his men, Ibrahim understood that the Spaniards were making a comeback in the ditch, and got ready for a counterattack. He got up to give the order to retreat but was immediately mowed down. His Bren-gun was silent. As he had not appointed anyone to replace him, the fourteen survivors stampeded in confusion, and instead of covering each other, broke formation and perished one after another under concentrated Spanish fire from the troops, which had scrambled out of the ditch and were advancing along the flat terrain. Lemkisser had managed to flee along a slope which led him to an overgrown thicket. He slipped between the foliage and from his hiding place with a long branch torn off a bush rubbed out the traces of his steps in the sand around the bush. A wise precaution, for when the Spanish soldiers reached the level where he was, they decided to go no further, believing that there were no more survivors.

They were not far from wrong. Lemkisser was the sole survivor. At night he ran off to seek an encampment that would give him shelter. He came back to the battle site the next day with two of his friends, and they proceded to bury the nineteen casualties. Their weapons had been taken by the Spaniards. He learned later that during the fight the Spaniards had suffered five dead and ten wounded out of the forty men in the two military vehicles. "They died like heroes," concluded Lemkisser. "And, as everyone knows, we come from Allah, and we shall go to join Him."

All the men present repeated those words. Then Salah, who had not uttered a word during this account, and by whose face not a single muscle had flinched, asked in a toneless voice, "That Mahmoud who got a bullet in the forehead—who exactly was he?"

He doubtless had already guessed the answer, but his heart had rejected what his mind had already understood, with a force, determination, and power that destroyed him like a man sinking under water.

"But it was your son, my Lord."

"No, that's impossible. May Allah curse those who lie," Salah added tonelessly.

"I assure you, my Lord. I'm ready to swear on the Koran." A heavy and seemingly endless silence ensued in which one could hear the buzzing of flies sailing about the room, and the rapid click of small beads. Suddenly, as though awakening from a dream, Salah rose up, tore off the turban covering his head, and cried out in a thundering voice,

"Assassins! You are assassins! You, Lemkisser! You, Ibrahim! And the other chiefs, your commanders!"

He made as if to get up and throw himself at Lemkisser, who did not budge. Ten hands were outstretched to restrain Salah, clutching at his robe. He sat down, took a breath, and continued.

"Not only are you imbeciles, you're also criminals. To send young inexperienced men to lay an ambush for hardened troops—that smacks of crime. Do you know whom you're dealing with? Men of the 'Bandera de la muerte,' the 'death battalions,' selected for their courage, endurance, discipline, trained for combat as well as the men of the French Foreign Legion. Poor imbeciles! You wanted to get them—twenty against forty! Vanquish and massacre the enemy. It's *they* who massacred you! But it's you who are responsible for Mahmoud's death—because of your stupidity. I solemnly demand reparations before Allah."

At those words a murmur of protest ran through the group. But Moulay Mehdi, overcome, told the protesters to be silent. Salah's anger was good; it was the natural outlet of any man of action; it was healthy.

Salah looked haggard. His eyes started from their sockets and his mouth frothed like that of a horse flayed by its bit during a race. He wiped his lips with the back of his sleeve and continued.

"War isn't made for amateurs. Believe me, in my youth I laid ambushes for Oulad Bousbaa with my father. We took precautions. When we attacked we checked in advance on the numbers of our enemies. If we were four against one, then the order for combat was given, and we were victorious. But if our numbers were less, or even equal to that of our adversaries, we did everything possible to avoid combat. Making war means killing the enemy, not getting yourself killed by him. Making war means winning, not risking defeat. You were twenty amateurs against forty professionals. Your number should have been four times that size to attack the Spaniards. That is the lesson to be learned from that stupid battle in which my son Mahmoud died through your fault, gentlemen of the Liberation Army, brainless gentlemen, defeated gentlemen!"

He was through. Moulay Mehdi and several of his companions were weeping like children, not trying to hold back their tears. Salah took a hold of himself. Not a tear would drop from his eyes in front of this crowd, not a single one. He felt grief spreading through his bones, his marrow, like a tidal wave. He thought he was losing his reason, and felt his head exploding. He had only one thought: to leave with dignity. He got up and called for his driver. Without a word, stiff and tall, he headed for the door, his step abrupt as a robot's. At the door, which led out onto the square, he turned around, in a few brief words told the crowd which wanted to accompany him that he wanted to be alone, and sank into the Mercedes.

When he arrived at the tent he saw Minatou, the old black servant whom his wife, Meriem, had given him five years earlier when he had left for Morocco. Minatou, who had raised his children, had been in his service for years now, and was tall and gaunt. She was intelligent. She had spread out the rugs on the mats, put milk in the calabashes, and laid out dates on the other side of the tent. She rushed out to meet him and understood from the look on his face that a misfortune had occurred. Looking straight into his eyes, she said, questioningly, "Mahmoud?"

"Yes," answered Salah. "Close the tent and go. I want to be alone." The servant, tears running down her bony face, obeyed quickly, and with nimble hands lowered the underflap of the tent, closing off all exits; then she fled, running as fast as she could into the countryside.

Alone at last, with no one there, Salah fell face forward to the ground, his arms crossed. He felt pain flood over him, pain too long bottled up. Many tears rolled down, flooding his face and the rug onto which he had collapsed. Huge sobs shook his body. The sound of his weeping, carried by the evening wind, united like an echo with those of Minatou. Sitting on the sands of the *wadi*, she rocked her torso back and forth, striking the ground with her head, calling Mahmoud's name in her laments, lacerating her cheeks with her nails, like the hired mourners of ancient times.

CHAPTER XX

For two months Salah lived in his tent like a wolf in its
cavern. All the efforts of his relatives and friends to see him
were in vain. He let no one in. His servant Minatou was the
only one who could talk to him. Twice a day she brought him
fresh milk and dates, sometimes clean clothes, a bit of steamed
semolina, and without saying a word vigilantly stood on guard
at the tent to ward off the curious. After the first few days there
were fewer visits, and Salah finally had time to think. He spent
the days prostrate, rosary, or rather *chapelet* in hand, to spell
the name of "Allah" for each bead. When night came he read
whole pages of the Koran under his breath as he had done in
his youth before his master, on whose block, with the tip of his

212

reed dipped into thick black ink, he had laboriously inscribed the verses learned during the daily lesson. He scrupulously recited the five daily prayers, the only times at which he could be seen leaving his tent. Usually, after the evening ablutions, he launched into the call to prayers as though he were at the same time a muezzin and an imam, and his voice, broken by sobs, rose up to heaven fresh and pure.

Prayer, reading the Koran, the silent ministrations of the worthy Minatou, were the only comforts for his immense sorrow.

Mahmoud's death felt like an open wound which would never fully heal. A month after this misfortune he had a surprise; he received from a camel-driver who came from Algeria a series of letters which deeply touched him. They came from Commander Larcher and his officers; Lieutenant Vogel, De Vignandeau and de La Renaudie. All of these officers, who had left Tindouf, were scattered throughout Algeria. Larcher was on the general staff of Colomb-Béchar, de Vignandeau guard commander of Tabelbala, de La Renaudie in the Aures, and Vogel in the Constantines in the East Hodna. Having heard the sad news, each of them reacted in his own way, forgetting their grievances against him. These officers, sensitive to the grief of a father, had found words of friendship which went right to his heart. Larcher, as usual, had spoken as a man of reason. He did not want, in such sad circumstances, to fail to extend to him his deepest sympathy, in the name of that old friendship which had formerly bound them. He explained that he had not approved of his departure for Morocco, but that he had understood the reasons for it. And here he held no rancor. He told him that General de Gaulle's coming to power had brought about the independence of many African states and that this doubtless would be the case for Algeria. Indeed, Salah knew that intensive negotiations had begun in Evian in France between representatives of the Algerian resistance and the French authorities which would lead to peace. Finally Larcher, though not wanting to interfere in the internal policies of the Reguibat, strongly advised him to return to Algeria and to his encampment to take in hand the confederation which he had abandoned during five years of voluntary exile in Morocco. The time had come when he had to think of his people first, of his family, of the Reguibat collective, now somewhat at a loss following the successive independence of Morocco, Mauritania, and now Algeria.

On a different scale, Vogel's letter also was very touching. The former officer-interpreter told him how deeply he sorrowed at the death of Mahmoud, whom he had found at Ain Ben Tili after the problem with the Sellam. He had a kind word for each member of his family, men and women; he even mentioned the name of his wife Meriem, and recalled the memory of Salambouha, his second wife and the mother of Mahmoud, with infinite tact.

One evening as he was reciting the prayer at sundown he turned around sharply and saw a man behind him following him in his prayers. His bearing was bold. He had barely finished the customary thanks to the angels accompanying him, when he called to the nomad. He then introduced himself, unabashed. He was Obeid Allahi, one of Salah's faithful men whose company he had much appreciated a few years ago. Obeid Allahi, who was from an outstanding family from Sidi Allal, was an attractive figure. A remarkable story-teller and highly intelligent, he knew how to win over his entourage by his brilliant answers and by a very special talent, that of divination. He read lines in the palm of the hand, was undefeated in interpreting celestial signs, passed himself off as a medium, and cured dislocated limbs by a mere touch. Salah had hired him as a secretary for several years, and had found him to be interesting and entertaining. Then one day the young man left him, giving various pretexts. This evening he had come back to show him, in his own way, the sympathy he felt

for him. Cut off from the world for two months, out of weakness or fatigue, Salah received Obeid Allahi into his tent and
thus bit by bit reacquired a taste for life.

This convalescence was immediately known in Goulimine.
The Governor several times had tried to meet Salah and was
getting more impatient by the day. For more than a month
now he had had an envelope with a large sum of money, which
the king had given him for Salah on learning of Mahmoud's
death, along with a very warm note of condolence. Now,
through Moulay Mehdi and Obeid Allahi, he managed to be
received in the tent by Salah. Salah had laid down his conditions; he did not want his tent invaded by a crowd of the
curious. At the appointed time, therefore, the Governor
arrived, accompanied by only his close counselors. Salah
received his guests politely but without displaying great enthusiasm. The visitors were struck by the change they found in the
chief of the Reguibat. He seemed to have aged ten years in two
months. He had gotten much thinner, his face was worn, his
hair had turned white, and his usually spirited gaze seemed
unseeing, as though permanent tears were fixed on the pupils.

After the traditional three cups of tea, during which the
conversation was limited to an exchange of views on the health
of all present and on weather conditions, the Governor took
the floor in his customary pompous style to present the condolences of his king. He gave Salah a letter from His Majesty,
which Salah read attentively. He thanked the Governor, and
requested him to transmit to the king his greetings, his deep
respect, and assurances of his total devotion. Then he fell
silent.

The hardest part remained for the Governor. He hesitated
for a long time, given the cold welcome shown him by Salah,
and finally extended to him an enormous envelope which
clearly contained many bank notes.

"His Majesty," he said, "knows fully well that a sum of
money, no matter how great, cannot replace the loss of a dear

one. But the king thought it might be of assistance to you in reconstituting part of your flocks which have been decimated by drought, and asks that you kindly accept it."

Salah continued telling his rosary beads and pretended not to have understood. He did not take the envelope, which the Governor continued to hold out to him, and this made the scene look absurd. Finally he spoke to thank the representative of the administration. He too believed that the loss of a dear one had no price, and if the drought had destroyed part of his flock, abundant rains would help them later. There was therefore no reason to accept such a sum. He had been sufficiently indulged by His Majesty in the past, he did not wish again to tax his generosity. He therefore suggested that this sum be used to indemnify the families of those who had died in the service of Morocco. For his part, he saw no use in it and therefore refused to take it.

Furious at having failed in his mission, the Governor took leave of Salah rather coolly.

A week after this meeting the sovereign Mohammed V died. Salah was profoundly moved. He wrote a telegram of condolences to Prince Moulay Hassan, but declined the Governor's invitation to come again to Rabat to present his best wishes to the new king.

It was then that Salah received a letter from Meriem, his wife, asking him to come back. Their encampment then was in Iguidi. The three married daughters were leading happy lives. His grandsons and granddaughters were doing well. One of them, wrote Meriem, looked like Mahmoud. She was sure he would like him. Why remain for no reason in a foreign country rather than be surrounded by the affection of his family? she concluded. That warm and tender letter upset him. That very evening he summoned Obeid Allahi and asked him about a way to return to Algeria in the most discreet manner possible. The most important thing was to get to Tindouf, and from there take a camel and reach the encampment.

Always ingenious, Obeid Allahi managed to hire an experienced tradesman named Hamoud from Goulimin. He knew Tindouf well because he had spent much time there on several occasions. Hamoud had a truck which he filled with sacks of sugar and chests of tea. One morning, at dawn, Salah, leaving behind his tent and servant so as not to arouse suspicion— he had promised Minatou that later he would send a camel-driver for her—got into the truck with Obeid Allahi next to the driver. Hamoud was a voluble Moroccan, very excited at the idea of going to Algeria when in principle the road was still closed. Salah and Obeid Allahi had thought that the French soldiers at the frontier post of Oum El Achar would let them through if they presented themselves as who they were. France had other worries at that time, as the Evian negotiations with the FLN, which had begun two months ago, continued. Moreover, the new king was about to embark on new struggles on the southern border to get rid of the French, who were in the process of negotiating Algeria's independence.

Once they had made their way to the border post without difficulty, the somewhat flabbergasted sentinel questioned the driver, who asked to speak to his lieutenant. The latter, who had just arrived from France, listened to the explanation Hamoud gave in French and sent a message by radio to Tindouf to find out whether he should let the truck through. He stressed that in the truck was an allegedly high-ranking individual named Salah ould Ahmed, who claimed that he was chief of the Reguibat confederation and who was on his way to Tindouf following a death in his family. The French authorities' reply came an hour later. The order was given to the lieutenant to let the truck through. Doubtless, he had made a mistake in giving the person's name. This wasn't Salah ould Ahmed, who was unknown, but Ahmed ould Salah, who at the present time was the chief of the Reguibat. When that reply was translated to Salah it made him smile. In less than five years the administration had forgotten him, and only knew his

French military post of Oum El Achar.

son, into whose hands he had entrusted interim command of the tribe. The lesson was a bitter one. Today, though, it had an advantage. The confusion in the names let him cross the border without difficulty.

The truck, which was not very new, set off on the last part of the winding road of Merkala with great difficulty. Then, in first gear it reached the Hamada, which extended as far as the eye could see. The driver stopped to let the motor cool down.

Getting out of the truck with difficulty, Salah was dazzled by the late afternoon light. He took deep breaths of the air of the plateau. A brilliant sun illuminated the tiniest details of this immense space, highlighting the young shoots on the pasture-land which, since there had been abundant rain the month before, were growing thickly and closely, like an enormous green fleece. The young grass shivered in a light wind. Salah left his companions and walked straight ahead for a few hundred meters. A small, hollow stretch wound through the thorns. He took off his shoes. The sand was already cool under his feet and the crushed grass was soft to the touch. Salah sat down cross-legged. For the first time since Mahmoud's death he felt a deep joy, which slowly grew into a feeling that was difficult to contain. He was getting younger. Finally, he once again was treading the land of his ancestors. He bent to the ground and buried his hand in the humid soil.

The palm of his hand was damp when he removed it. The rain that had fallen had gone beyond the level of the fingers to reach the center of his hand. The grass therefore had to be growing abundantly. The flocks were going to have a feast, and the she-camels would give a lot of foaming milk, redolent of all the scents of the earth.

He suddenly remembered that the time for the afternoon prayer had come. He sat down and stretched himself out. He heard the sound of the wind passing through the plants, giving off its typical hushing sound, and the dull sound of the tea glasses clinking against the sugar loaf announcing the tea that his companions were preparing. He felt at ease. He lay down in the hollow of the dale, his head facing the sky. The tears came to his eyes, but they were sweet and he did not try to hold them back. He had to accept the death of two beings he had held dear, for such was the will of Allah. He thought of Salambouha, his beloved wife, his great love, once again, he asked her to forgive him for not having been able to keep Mahmoud alive. But perhaps his son in paradise would be united with his mother and hand in hand they would go down the lanes of the marvelous gardens with their singing cascades.

He got up, turned toward the east, and prepared to start the call to prayer. But he delayed uttering the cry of "Allahou Akbar," "Allah is the greatest." In the calm sky of perfect blue a round cloud, enormous and awkward, was coming down the slopes of the Atlas Mountains and heading off like a child's balloon towards the south. Glowing pink in the sun, it continued on its solitary path, doubtless preceding other clouds which in battle formation were planning to follow it. An advance sentinel, it seemed to be in a hurry, just like Salah, to be reunited with the sands of Iguidi, to bring it its beneficial showers. Thus, it was following the same road as Salah, who in that immense space recalled that, above all, he had remained a son of the clouds.